Ray Bolger defies gravity in Where's Charley?, *a musical adaptation of* Charley's Aunt, *October 11, 1948, at the St. James Theatre.*

SHOW BUSINESS IS NO BUSINESS

BY AL HIRSCHFELD

SIMON AND SCHUSTER   NEW YORK

MANUFACTURED IN THE UNITED STATES OF AMERICA
PRINTED BY REEHL LITHO COMPANY, NEW YORK
BOUND BY H. WOLFF BOOK MFG. COMPANY, NEW YORK

To my wife, Dolly Haas

I wish to acknowledge my indebtedness to the proprietors of the New York *Times* and *Holiday* for kindly allowing me to reproduce some of the drawings in this book which originally appeared in their pages.

CONTENTS

INTRODUCTION

Some thirty years ago two bland black eyes appeared on the American theatrical scene, peering out from above a neat black beard, giving the picture of a small boy staring over a well-tended hedge. They were guileless black eyes, almost lamblike, and they gave the impression that they were seeing our theatre in the soft light of love and affection.

Soon there began to appear in our newspapers and magazines caricatures drawn by the sensitive hands beneath the eyes and the beard. If these had been studied closely, they might well have been the tip-off. They were brilliant caricatures, distinguished first of all by unmistakable signs that they were the work of a fine artist. They were at once reportorial and imaginative. They were cunning, too, with a crafty, vulpine, unreal approach to the real.

But because of their subtlety it was difficult to imagine just what those bland, black eyes really were seeing.

That difficulty no longer exists. Al Hirschfeld, the man whose eyes they are, has written the book you are about to read. In these pages he reveals, with no such subtlety as his caricatures contained, that what his mind was drinking in was not the world of glamour and gaiety that the theatre is thought to be by all of you on the dark side of the footlights. Here is the cynic's guidebook to the world of make-believe.

If I had read Show Business Is No Business *before I plunged like a mad thing into the theatre back in the Polk administration, I probably would have taken up covered-wagon repair work and would today be a happy mechanic instead of neurology's pet. For Mr. Hirschfeld's chapter on "Playwrights" alone, written as it is in his own blood, will save many an aspiring dramatist from a fate worse than bad motives.*

He pays his respects with equivalent contumely to the producer, the director, the actor, the designer, and the agent. He blasts the ghastly practice of auditioning actors, from which the most to be gained is the knowledge that they speak English, and the equally ghastly audition for angels, omitting only the story of one such goings on at which the producer not only did not raise a single dollar toward his impending production but also had his umbrella stolen. And he does not spare the out-of-town opening, where everyone agrees cheerfully "It needs a lot of work," or the New York première, where the audience assembles to be seen and not to see.

All of this is written with cynical humor and fine sarcastic bite. Most artists cannot even spell. It is not only a surprise but a great joy to find one who can really write.

—RUSSEL CROUSE

THEATRES

"THE GERM of the theatre as it arose among the Greeks was the paved *orchestra,* or circular dancing place, for the performance of the choric dances in the worship of Dionysus. The altar stood in the middle, and the open auditorium, which in Greek theatres is always built on the side of a hill, rose in tiers of stone seats (traversed by open aisles radiating from the center) in a semicircular shape about it. The theatre at Athens is said to have held nearly thirty thousand persons. . . . The drama of the Middle Ages was performed in temporary booths by traveling players. . . . With the revival of the secular drama the first permanent playhouse in London was erected by and licensed to the father of Richard Burbage, the actor, in 1576-1577, and was soon followed by the famous Globe Theatre (identified with Shakespeare) and others. Wooden structures were gradually replaced by structures of stone, and in the last part of the seventeenth century scenery was introduced."

This is as far as the editors of Funk and Wagnalls' New Standard Dictionary of the English language take up their findings on the word "theatre." Perhaps they are justified in omitting any reference to the eighteenth and nineteenth centuries in their report, but now that we are past the halfway mark in the twentieth century, it seems to me about time they realized that something new has been added. I offer the following facts to the editors of Funk and Wagnalls without charge (except a small, reasonable royalty and pension plan, which I would pre-

*Intermission,
Broadway style*

fer discussing directly with Funk and Wagnalls and my agent) should they decide to include in their *New* New Dictionary these pertinent facts which would bring their cultural record of the theatre up to date.

The Broadway theatre is a real-estate development in Art. The owners of the theatres and the producers of the shows that fill them have nothing in common except a lease.

Theatres have become unpredictable personalities, reflecting the popularity of the current shows playing in them. A theatre presenting three flops in a row automatically becomes a jinx house, while another, by virtue of a series of smash hits, will earn for itself the accolade of lucky house. The reputations of theatres, like the actors who inhabit them, are subject to change without notice. A lucky house, presenting the prevailing first lady of the theatre in a play written by America's most cele- brated playwright, is well on its way to becoming a jinx house with a second-rate actress playing in a stinker written by a hack, when their combined efforts are greeted with oppugnant re- sponse from the press and audience.

These neurotic buildings, sprinkled from Thirty-ninth to Fifty-ninth Street, are to be found not further than two blocks off Broadway. Theatres located beyond this inflexible boundary are arbitrarily designated as "off-Broadway," or "experimental," theatres. The Miller, Hellinger, Playhouse, Mansfield, Hudson, Lyceum, Alvin, Empire, Forty-eighth, Center, Beck, and Bilt- more Theatres are all privately owned. The Forty-sixth, Fulton, Morosco, and Coronet Theatres are the properties of the City Investment Corporation. Everything else in New York (with the possible exceptions of a few small parks and a couple of subway lines) belongs to the Shuberts.

With the passing of the Theatre Guild Playhouse into the clutches of radio and video, there remains but one theatre on Broadway as the sole survivor of an earlier tradition: the Hel- linger Theatre. This theatre, owned by Mr. Anthony B. Farrell, devotes itself exclusively to the productions of its owner-man- ager.

Mr. Farrell, an Albany boy, is a recent convert to the ulcer- loving folk of show business. He comes to Broadway with a huge personal fortune accumulated through years of hard work and the diligent banking of tremendous wads of money bequeathed to him by deceased relatives. (The late "Diamond Jim" Brady was one of his many illustrious uncles.) Mr. Farrell's advent into show business started with a modest investment of three hundred thousand dollars in a musical revue titled *All for Love*. He subsequently found it expedient to purchase a million-dollar theatre to play it in.

Intermission, experimental-theatre style

The purchase of the theatre turned out to be specifically just that and nothing more. Mr. Farrell bought the Hollywood Theatre from the Warner Brothers, rechristened it the Hellinger

Anthony B. Farrell

Theatre, and then discovered that he did not own the smoking lounge or the lobby.

This strange state of affairs was further aggravated by the fact that the owners of the smoking lounge and the lobby could not be persuaded to part with these odd bits of real estate. The smoking lounge, owned by the Fifty-first Street Corporation, and the lobby, owned by the Emery Estate, conjured up sentimental attachments and emotional ties hallowed by sordid memories, attachments too strong to be severed for mere mercenary consideration.

The ordinary unimaginative citizen, confronted with these seemingly insurmountable conditions, would have given up at this point, but not Mr. Farrell. In a typically Yankee deal, which completely escapes the average drone, Mr. Farrell managed to overcome both of these obstacles by paying a yearly fee of forty thousand dollars to the Fifty-first Street Corporation for inhaling rights in the smoking lounge, and another forty thousand dollars per annum to the Emery Estate for the "right of way" through the lobby. This fiendishly clever device, put over by Mr. Farrell, allows the theatre patrons to go in and out of the theatre through the front door.

Of course, this arrangement leaves the Fifty-first Street Corporation and the Emery Estate with the potential power to trap a large segment of Manhattan's population in a sealed and well-furnished mausoleum. But in the event of such an unlikely situation arising, I have no doubt that Mr. Farrell would personally rescue his audience by some ingenious method, making the exploits of Monte Cristo seem like kid stuff by comparison.

Among the "off-Broadway" theatres there also is only one theatre owned and operated exclusively for its own productions: the Davenport Free Theatre, on East Twenty-seventh Street. Mr. Butler Davenport's Free Theatre has withstood the vicissitudes of two world wars and eight mortgage foreclosures during its thirty-seven years of existence.

True to the implication of its name, there is never an admission charge at Mr. Davenport's Free Theatre. He has managed to maintain his one-man art project on a purely religious basis by merely passing the plate after each performance. This *lais-*

sez-faire system has achieved what well may be some kind of permanent record in the American theatre, for it has made possible the production by Mr. Davenport, in which he also plays

Butler Davenport

the leading role, of the longest-running play in the history of the American theatre. The play is *The Bells,* adapted for Henry Irving by Leopold Lewis from the original German play *The Story of the Polish Jews,* by Erckmann-Chatrian. Produced in London in 1871 and later made into a silent movie starring Harry Bauer, it has remained for Mr. Davenport to exploit in this country. He built the sets and moved into them thirty-six years ago. Year after year, ever since 1914, *The Bells* and Mr. Davenport have consistently played to slightly bewildered audiences in his Free Theatre.

The rental of a Broadway theatre is more or less standardized. The lessee or producer, in return for a minimum guarantee —a percentage of the gross and a pint of blood—is given a heated or cooled theatre, depending on the weather. It also includes house lighting, a box-office staff, house manager, ushers, cleaning women, porters, front and backstage doormen, night watchman, engineer, master carpenter, property man, electrician, a "fly man," whose sole contribution to our time is the raising and lowering of the asbestos house curtain, ice for the water coolers, hatcheck personnel, the tickets, and toilet paper.

The percentage of the gross demanded for these formidable services is variable. The "well-known," "famous," or "established" producers (see chapter on "Producers") are tapped on the basis of past performances. A luckless producer may have to give, along with an inflated slice of the take, a percentage of the show itself. This naturally would include the potential revenue from road companies, radio and television rights, and movie sale.

Apart from the revocable license which every theatre must maintain in order to stay in business, the City of New York enforces a special building code applicable only to theatre construction. This code restricts the height of the building to the height of the theatre. The roof of the theatre must be the roof of the building. No offices, apartments, or other income-producing rooms may be constructed over the theatre. The superstition persists that a theatre is a giant crematorium and all who enter do so at their own peril.

It is difficult to understand the wisdom of a law which allows restaurants with their own fire-making equipment—such as gas stoves, open hearth fires, grills, rotisseries, blazing shashlik, and flaming crêpes Suzettes—to carry on their business in a crowded office building while a fireproof building constructed over a fireproof theatre is condemned as a fire trap. It seems unreasonable to assume that an unprotected filing clerk, barbecued in his office over a flaming Chinese restaurant, prefers this type of cookery to being fried in his office over a blazing theatre. Yet these are the facts restricting the construction of new theatres. Office buildings are allowed to be burned only by restaurants, not theatres.

These discriminatory regulations imposed by the City Fathers, plus increased taxes and reduced prices of admission (theatre tickets for a musical in 1928 were six-sixty top; today similar tickets cost six dollars. The net to the management after extracting Federal tax was six dollars in 1928 and today it amounts to five dollars), explain in no way the fact that our theatres today make a hell of a lot of money.

2

PRODUCERS

In the theatre everybody is a genius except the producer.

The producer cannot write a play, neither can he direct a play, and he has no money; but without him the theatre could not exist.

To be a producer you need only to say, "I am a producer."

To be a "well-known" producer it is necessary to get this statement printed as many times as possible in the Broadway columns.

To be an "established" producer you will have to produce a play.

To be a "great" or "famous" producer you will have to produce a successful play.

Let us assume you have taken the plunge by casually announcing, "I am a producer." You will be well on your way to becoming a "well-known" producer if this casual announcement is made within earshot of a literary agent, and, besides, all your lunch tabs for the ensuing weeks will automatically be taken care of. On your first visit to Sardi's, with the agent bearing a manuscript in a bright green cover, you will be amazed at the solicitous interest everyone will have in you. Renée, the hat-check girl, will immediately try to check the manuscript with your hat. Your agent, aware of these harmless attempts at espi-

"A producer"

onage, will snatch the manuscript back, introducing you by name and your new title, "a producer." This horseplay in the coatroom practically assures you of an item in the gossip columns. When this item appears, you henceforth will be referred to as "a well-known producer."

Not being able to afford a phone establishes you in the theatre as a man of great wealth, inaccessible, not of the cheap

A "well-known" producer

Broadway mob; a serious, learned sort of chap. "Is it true that you are dickering with Charlie Chaplin and Greta Garbo to co-star in your coming vehicle?" (A vehicle in the theatre is a play, never a bicycle.) "Will Josh Logan direct?" "We understand Howard Cullman is trying to get a piece of your show."

You will discover, after many years, your reputation may wane. The columnists will tire of you, not because the rumors about you have all been false but because other "well-known" producers, younger and with more active inertia, are crowding you into the has-been class. Sympathy, the curse of Broadway, may plague you. "Grand old man. Talented as all hell, but he seems to have lost his touch." You are now touching bottom. But do not be discouraged. No one ever got anywhere in the theatre without staging a comeback. *You* are now ready for yours.

To reawaken lagging interest in your activities it is advisable to establish a "foundation" bearing your name. The two salient features of this foundation need in no way differ from other foundations: first, the encouragement of artists and poets; second, the perpetuation of your name.

There being no group in the whole world more amenable to encouragement than the artists and poets, the foundation will have no trouble enlisting their enthusiastic support.

The perpetuation of your name can be arranged through a "sponsoring committee." This committee, chosen from the world's greatest minds, with a sprinkling of statesmen, dictators, and a fellow by the name of Zorach, will consider itself singly honored to serve.

The ostensible purpose of the sponsoring committee of the foundation would be to select, from the avalanche of manuscripts submitted, the most promising American playwright, between the ages of thirty and thirty-six, blond, clean-shaven, married, and unpublished, to be the winner of your annual award—a gold-plated theatre mask.

Editorial columns in leading newspapers will champion your cause; playwrights will shower you with scripts that have been rejected by every amateur group on both coasts; ghost-written articles for national magazines and radio and television appearances will pay your weekly room rent for years to come. There is, however, a gimmick to all this, for, as we all know, nothing is ever obtained in this life without paying a price. You, as producer, are no exception to this inexorable rule. You must now actually produce a play. There is no way out for you. May as well face it like a man.

Up till now you have invested nothing except a reckless acceptance of the theatre and a gold-plated mask. Don't try to be

An "established" producer

sensible and retire at this stage of your career. You have passed the chicken-liver phase and are well on your way toward the Baked Alaska. Your gambling instinct, plus a confused sense of your debt to the public, will help you select a script for production.

The outcome of this production will automatically stamp you as an "established" producer, even though your vehicle

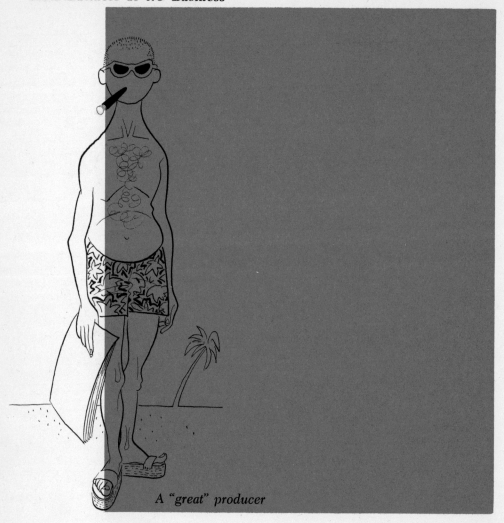

A *"great" producer*

opens and closes on the same night; the unhappy play that opens to rave notices and runs for eighteen months with fluctuating profit and loss on alternate weeks, finally closing with a clear, undisputed loss of sixty thousand dollars for the backers, will earn you the accolade of "famous" producer; should your efforts produce a smash hit, your closest enemies will be forced to admit you into the ranks of "great" producer. There is really nothing to worry about; you have nothing to lose except your amateur standing.

After all, in the event of an out-and-out stinker, the Street realizes that you didn't write the play and no one in his right mind would accuse or blame you for the monstrous acting which took place on the stage. . . . No, you are absolutely in the clear.

On the other hand, *if* (and it does happen occasionally) you find yourself with a smash hit after the notices come out, do not be surprised if the city government, industrialists, publishers, bankers, artists and poets, and your landlord come to you for advice. You are definitely the man of the hour. Let's face it. Where would the theatre be without you?

No one can accurately predict the success of any production after reading the manuscript or witnessing the completed play on the stage. Your guess is as good as anyone else's. There are no exceptions and there are no experts.

A few seasons ago I saw a run-through of a revival of *R.U.R.* at the Ethel Barrymore Theatre. This play, written by Karel Capek, was originally done by the Theatre Guild in 1922 and deals with the future of mankind and the inherent evils of manufacturing neurotic robots. Daniel Blank and David Silberman were the producers of the revival. They were seated out front in the empty auditorium, Blank with a Lily cup full of rye and Silberman holding the bottle. On stage was Lee Strasberg, one of the theatre's genuinely gifted directors, showing a mob of extras how to walk like robots. As the plot unfolded, it became increasingly clear to me that Mr. Capek, the author, preferred mad scientists to golems. As for myself, I have always liked juicy blondes, and so the whole problem of whether or not the animated beer cans or the lunatic with the wig took over this planet became a matter of complete indifference to me. My interest focused itself on Blank and Silberman, who sat there bug-eyed watching the drama taking place on stage. They were visibly moved by every nuance in the play, laughing and weeping and refilling their Lily cups as the afternoon wore on. At the final curtain, they arose as one man and threw their arms around each other. Spilling over with emotion, they congratulated the cast, the director, and each other. Convinced they had just seen a play that would run longer than the combined runs of *Abie's Irish Rose* and *Life with Father,* they assigned me to design a robot that could be used for paperweights, salt shakers, automobile radiator caps, and sundry other utilitarian *objets d'art.* Long-range advertising projects were immediately discussed. The press agent was alerted to shoot the works. This was it. *R.U.R.* was not going to be just another highly successful play on Broadway. The plans were to make it an American institution.

R.U.R. opened the following week and was hammered by the critics. It closed after four performances. I wound up with a paperweight of a golem I had designed. I don't know what became of Blank. Silberman went back to his former business, where I understand he is known as the Zipper King.

In earlier, more carefree days, the producer could oversubscribe his show by selling half-interests to as many suckers as he could find. By way of example—let us assume that a producer sold forty thousand dollars' worth of shares in a ten-thousand-dollar production, or four hundred per cent of the production's actual cost. He would then have to pay back to the investors four dollars for every dollar of profit taken in at the box office. Needless to say, this type of disastrous success rarely took place, for it then became the producer's inclement function, in those halcyon days, to destroy whatever chances of success the play may have had. An enraged citizenry in combination with various theatrical unions and police organizations put an end to this flowering of the free-enterprise system. The theatre has remained legitimate ever since. (See next chapter.)

Your lawyer, following the ethics of his profession and the threat of disbarment, will prevent you from using any of the money on deposit in your special account until every last penny of the estimated budget is safely in the till. The fun of just letting the stuff trickle through your fingers will be denied to you. Having seventy-five thousand of an estimated eighty-thousand-dollar budget stashed away in a bank, and not a dime in cash for an immediate cup of coffee, can be pretty exasperating. This pent-up frustration nurtured during feverish months of auditioning for angels will disappear on the day all the money is in. It will not be necessary for you to make a formal announcement of the fact that you are finally in business. The *Wall Street Journal* will automatically list your corporation or limited partnership in its columns along with the name and individual investment of each subscriber. Unfortunately, this paper will be read only by your backers. To establish definitely your new status on Broadway, it will be necessary for you to choose one or all of the following suggestions:

1. Don't answer your phone.
2. Initial your shirts.
3. Carry a money clip with new bills in it.
4. Fly to Hollywood for the weekend.
5. Divorce your wife or, if this is inconvenient, never take her out in public again.
6. Get married.
7. Invite another producer to your table at Sardi's and pay the bill.

PLAYRIGHTS

THIS IS a chapter on what to do after you have written a play.

(1) Mail yourself a sealed carbon copy of your manuscript. Deposit this, unopened, in your safety deposit box. Later, when you are sued for plagiarism, you can produce this sealed envelope in court. (The postmark will prove your priority by establishing the day you mailed it.) Unfortunately, it will not be admitted as evidence in your trial, but it's a good precaution to take just in case you are not sued. If this good fortune should befall you—and there are many precedents where a man has written a successful play and was not sued—you then have your original manuscript, still intact, and may sell it again as a new play. Don't forget, you are now two years older than when you first sold this play for an immediate production; you have rewritten it many times for the "experts" and by now you are thoroughly disgusted with it. The rereading of your original play will help restore your failing sanity: it will at once become apparent to you that the produced play in no way bears any resemblance to your original manuscript. Even your agent will have forgotten what the original play was about and will greet the old script with new enthusiasm.

(2) Practice in front of a mirror the formal manners of theatre speech. Remove the pipe from your mouth, extend an eager hand, bare your freshly capped teeth, keeping them firmly clamped together, and say, "Glad to meet you." Repeat this until you have mastered it. Then try "Marvelous," "Too wonderful," "Really," and "Isn't it?" using the same general technique. Now open your mouth wide, throw your head back, extend your arms to receive a completely strange woman who

will embrace you on meeting and scream, "Darling!" The trick here is to get your "Darling!" in before hers. This is not an easy thing to do, but it is worth the effort. You will be respected not only as a playwright but as a man of the theatre.

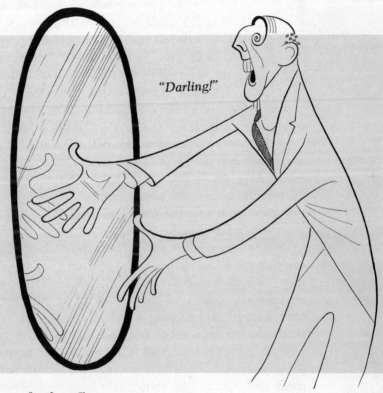

"Darling!"

(3) Learn to drink coffee.

(4) Never accept an invitation to a backer's home for dinner. He has invited you to make a few ill-chosen suggestions about the script.

(5) Don't try to discover new restaurants. Confine your eating to the 21, Sardi's, Lindy's, the Sixth Avenue Delicatessen, and other people's apartments. Never invite them to yours. Your receding hairline will be mistaken for a high brow if you remain aloof, mysterious, inaccessible.

(6) When impossible script revisions are suggested, try a

"Marvelous!" or "Too wonderful!" on them. Don't argue. Logic, normal reflexes, sanity, or any of the other attributes which distinguish man from the ape will avail you nothing in these hourly crises.

(7) Learn to accept the fact that if it weren't for your play the producers would have a smash hit on their hands. The bitter truth is that the least important thing, once the wheels of production have started turning, is the play you have written. As an example: It says in your script, "Herman enters—stage right—his arms laden with toys for his wife." Opening night of your play: Herman enters—stage right—steps on the freshly waxed stage and slides right across it, barely missing his wife, who makes a grab for the toys as he goes whizzing past. Herman disappears from view through the wings at stage left. His dizzy exit into the serpentined cables backstage, followed by a resounding crash into the "light control" switchboard, may darken the house and your career at the same time. The insignificance of your play compared with a stagehand who can't even wax a floor is at once apparent.

Playwrights suffer under the happy illusion that "the play's the thing." Admittedly—as the curtain rises in our theatres tonight. There would be no maids talking into dead telephones without the genius of our playwrights; no portable fireplace with a stagehand waving a sparkler behind it, warming an already perspiring actor in front of it; no hunting lodge equipped with its own thunder and lightning would normally entice an actor to shoot himself in it; no respectable married woman with three children would voluntarily become a rejected whore six nights a week, and every Wednesday and Saturday afternoon, without a script. None of these phenomena would be possible without the playwright. They are his inventions.

Everyone in the theatre will readily agree that "the play's the thing." That is, everyone except those with a play already in their hands. The play's waning importance will be felt by everyone as the production goes along. Even those whose writing up to that time had been confined to "Wish you were here" scribbled on a post card suddenly blossom as editors, critics, rewrite men, play doctors, and idea men. Once your play is written, you may as well resign yourself to the inevitable truth:

you are a layman among experts. Even sixteen-year-old girls have been in the business long before you were born.

The imperceptible change from "the play's the thing" to "the production's the thing" begins with nothing more serious than

The experts

a friendly, "Fine script, my boy. Just needs a little tightening." After a few weeks the "little tightening" comes to mean: eliminate "Onlookers" and "Cossacks" from the script—too impractical for the budget and, besides, they don't further the story; change the locale from Russia to Texas—it's more familiar to an audience and it would eliminate all those expensive costumes; an all-Negro cast would cut the payroll in half and give the play that extra something which, by this time, everyone

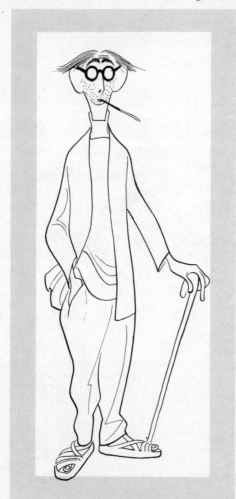

"feels" is lacking in the script. The difficult thing at this stage of the game is to react with interest to all of these inane suggestions, for they may be right. Remember: *Anna Lucasta* was originally written about a Polish family but by the time it reached Broadway it became a Negro problem play. Even Gilbert and Sullivan had their greatest success on Broadway with a "Hot" version of *The Mikado*. The all-Negro production of *Macbeth* sponsored by the Federal theatre was another notable revising of Shakespeare. Take comfort in the fact that if they can do it to Shakespeare they can do it to you.

Hollywood playwrights live in Bucks County.

Most proletarian playwrights live in penthous

Comedy playwrights live in brownstones.

Smart Set playwrights live in furnished rooms, and all other

playwrights live in Connecticut or High Tor, except Saroyan, who lives on Fifteenth Avenue in San Francisco. These playwrights established themselves before the housing shortage. Today the problem is more complex. Unless your play and your present address happily coincide with the above listing, I would advise you to rewrite to suit your present living quarters.

To evaluate your dubious position in the theatre, all you have to do is put yourself in the place of an apple. You are picked by the producer, polished by the director, packaged by the actors, transported by the business manager, sold by the press agent, and consumed by the public. There is very little you or the apple can do about it. Every commercial apple is similarly handled before the public has a chance to discover whether or not there is a worm in either of you.

4

DIRECTORS

A DIRECTOR is a man, woman, or child with an inordinate love of the theatre and money. Their genuine interest in the culture and welfare of the theatre is only natural, when you consider that top-flight directors get twenty per cent of the gross.

To become a director it is necessary to establish yourself as an authority on the subject. This may seem, at first glance, an insurmountable hurdle because of your inexperience. Do not let the detail of never having directed anything before deter you from your chosen field. Remember, all other directors were forced to start their careers with nothing more than a few well-chosen sentences on the subject as their sole recommendation.

Develop a negative personality. Let it be known that you are dissatisfied with the current trend in direction. Point out specific scenes from productions now running; show how ineptly they were directed and what you would have done with the same scenes. Most important of all is your ability to convince your potential patrons that one of the greatest evils in the theatre of today is the fact that *you* are not employed in it. Theatre folk respect this kind of integrity and, besides, you may be right.

There are schools for actors, playwrights, designers, and musicians, but none for directors. Yours is a nebulous art with limitless boundaries. You must be part designer, part playwright, part musician, and part actor, although it will never be necessary for you to try your skill professionally in any of these restricting art forms. The real art of the director is his ability to get a script to direct.

Once you have wheedled yourself into an assignment, the playwright, designer, and actors will be of inestimable help to you. These competent professionals will never doubt the superior authority vested in you as their director. They have been trained to carry out your most insane suggestions with ingenious resourcefulness. Everyone will be in awe of you, for you are the one man in the theatre whose finished work cannot be judged until it is too late. You will be creating your masterpiece right up to the night of the opening in New York. Sometimes directors keep on creating even after the closing notice has been pasted on the backstage bulletin board. No one really knows with any certainty whether you have made or broken the play.

Most successful directors are either playwrights or disillusioned actors. This is one of the rare fields in the theatre where being Hungarian is not enough.

The director's dubious art is perpetrated in public before a lot of people. He creates on the spur of the moment with unfailing omnipotence. Sometimes acting a scene with inner conviction, he will portray a beautiful woman—a grotesquerie for anyone to witness except other actors, who understand these insanities. The next moment he will transform himself (and for himself alone, as far as I'm concerned) into a robot, a boy scout, or a cackling old miser; all these impersonations are done with assurance and incompetence. Convinced of his mastery of these various roles, he then puts the actors through their paces. They are told to mimic his interpretations; each detail is carefully rehearsed until all the actors develop the peculiar mannerisms of the director. A really forceful director can leave his mark for years on a sensitive actor. When all the actors in a production begin to look, act, and talk like the director, the director has achieved what is known in the theatre as his thumbprint.

There are, of course, as many ways of directing a script as there are ways of painting a picture; the big difference is that no one will give you a couple of hundred thousand dollars to paint a picture.

Some directors direct by inference. A smile or a hurt look are the only visible signs of life in this type of director. He assumes the helpless approach: a beaten man with every hand in

The actor-director

the theatre set against him. These professional sulkers pouting in odd corners of the theatre are brought out of their shells by overzealous actors, whose only aim in life is to please them. This specie of director is usually a lovable fellow. His arrogant timidity instills a sense of responsibility in the actors. They simply cannot let him down; they feel they must come through for him —and they usually do.

Then there is the European director. This "Mittel-europaer" with a *gemütlich* accent is constantly preoccupied with correcting the actors' speech. Bundled up like a premature baby and seated in the darkened auditorium surrounded by a staff of as-

The European director

sistants, he may be heard delivering long harangues in broken English on the importance of diction in the theatre. He never goes on the stage to instruct his actors—they come down to him. Brooklyn boys, after a few weeks, may be seen clicking their heels before addressing the Herr Professor; the girls automatically extend their paws for the old man's lips. This Old World charm, which practically destroyed Central European culture, has about the same effect on the theatre over here. The maestro is constantly amused at the naïveté of the American theatre. New effects employing Lucite or television were used by him long before they were invented. He remembers, with pedantical accuracy, his production in the nineties of *The Flying Kreplach,* wherein he first predicted the discovery of atomic power. His wild talent demonstrates itself by being ahead or behind the times, but never part of it.

The typical Broadway director is the exact opposite of the European director. He prides himself on his business acumen. All Art is highly suspect to this padded-shouldered extrovert who cannot restrain himself from answering your questions before they are asked. His pep and assurance are depressing to more contemplative minds. Producers have unshakable faith in his talents because he thinks Einstein is a screwball. He is never at a loss for a solution, no problem exists that he cannot solve in a flash; he will fold his show immediately after the opening notices, and start with renewed vigor on another disaster. He knows what the public wants: sex and corn. The fact that the public stays away from his sure-fire productions in alarming numbers does not alter the preconceived ideas of this entrepreneur. He—in common with bankrupt Sixth Avenue art shops who overstocked their shelves with arty prints of "September Morn," "The Last Waterhole," and "The Storm"—is loaded down with unsalable notions. Even Woolworth's five- and ten-cent stores have recognized the public demand for van Gogh and Picasso, but the "commercial" director steadfastly refuses to accept Shakespeare. He is proud of his commercialism, insisting the theatre is big business. Yet his theatre, whose only interest is the rapid accumulation of contemporary money, has consistently operated at a loss for many years.

The Broadway director

The "experimental" director distinguishes himself by producing established classics and contemporary plays by prize-winning authors. A Hollywood star or two in the leading roles (symbolic of the revolt against the crass commercialism of the cinema industry) also help to give the whole thing an experimental air. The financial success of these experiments is doubly gratifying to the sponsors because they honestly believed in the

The "experimental" director

play. This lucrative field is surprisingly discovered toward the end of every theatrical season by the *dreamers*. Everyone connected with these productions works for minimum salary. The craft unions recognize the experimental nature of the enterprise; they generally make special concessions which allow their members to work below minimum scale. The theatre world is fundamentally sentimental and will shower all of its potential good will on these sound investments. The scenic designer is persuaded to cut his fee to half money and half prestige. Hollywood stars normally earning three thousand dollars a week will happily work for a hundred and a quarter, paying all their own transportation costs from the Coast. It is not uncommon for these experimental plays to move from their unventilated theatres in Greenwich Village up to the commercial theatres off Times Square. There salaries are boosted to normal; the scenic artist turns in his prestige receipt for cash, and the director-producer milks his well-earned dividends from the experiment.

AGENTS

THE PLAYWRIGHT'S agent gets ten per cent.

The Composer's agent gets ten per cent.

The Lyricist's agent gets ten per cent.

The Director's agent gets ten per cent.

The Actor's manager-agent gets ten per cent.

The Designer's agent gets ten per cent.

The Choreographer's agent gets ten per cent.

The Conductor's agent gets ten per cent.

The Advertising agent gets fifteen per cent.

The Angel's agent or "finder" gets ten per cent.

The Agent's agent works on a straight-salary basis.

DESIGNERS

To BE a designer in the theatre you must be able to recognize the difference between a great braguette and a G-string; a Tuscan pillar, an Ionic column, and a Brass Rail; Louis Quatorze and a Morris chair; El Greco and Tade Styka. You must also have five hundred dollars in cash.

Equipped with these essentials, plus an ability to make a drawing in perspective, you are eligible to join the Scenic Artists' Union, Local 829, an affiliate of the Paper Hangers' Union.

If you should pass the mental and financial tests and be accepted as a full-fledged member of this branch of the Paper Hangers' Union, the logical consequence of your folly may be that you will be one of those chosen few actually given an assignment to design the sets for a new play. The probability of either of these extravagant assumptions ever happening is about as remote as the growth of a small hand behind your ear.

But for the purposes of this chapter, let me abuse the privilege of being stupid and assume you are a member of the Scenic Artists' Union, with a script in front of you. It is an odds-on-even bet that the script is a one-set play which takes place in a living room. This locale, the favored haunt of playwrights, you may find a bit frustrating for your first assignment, but as time goes on, and your reputation grows, you will find it more frustrating.

Your original ambition to create a "space theatre" employing all the technical advances of modern science will disintegrate across the years like your teeth. The magic of Polaroid,

Lucite, and projection to create an illusion of reality may be your private dream which you will settle for publicly by using the standard "revolving bagel set" for quick scene changes. The expedient settlement, for practical reasons, usually boils down to an exquisitely furnished room whose functional furniture will serve the producer for many years in his own living room after the show closes.

A primary rule (and one you are not likely to find outside the pages of this book) is to find out what kind of furniture your producer likes—and design accordingly.

If it were not for this furniture fetish indulged in by the producer, the feasibility of constructing permanent living-room sets in a segregated theatre would have long since become a practical reality—a sort of "living-room theatre," dedicated to the one-set, living-room play. The potentialities of this specially

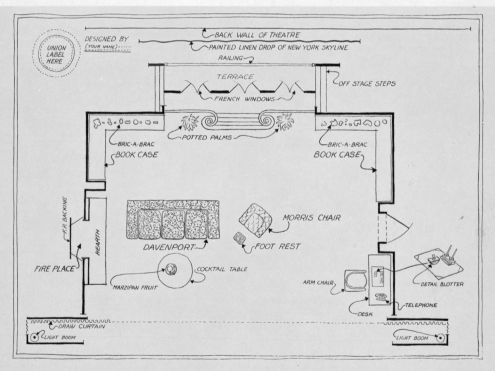

A "living-room theatre"

designed theatre (apart from the beneficial effect of quarantining the virus in one house) could be an endless source of inspiration to playwrights who never get out of their own living rooms. Adjustable wall surfaces to suit the most fastidious playwright could be adjusted with some sort of hook-and-eye device: mahogany panels for the Publisher, wallpaper for the Bronx Family, whitewashed brick for the Author, tapestries for the Philanthropist, velours for the Artist, stucco for the Honeymooners, and painted transparencies for the Dream Sequence. A property room stuffed with every kind of portable fireplace,

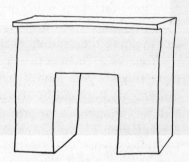

bookcase, doctor's diploma, umbrella stand, hat rack, bird cage, alpaca flower, mounted fish, antlers, and marzipan fruit.

Unfortunately there has been a trend during the past hundred and fifty years toward more elaborate windows and doors. The "living-room theatre," with its limited supply of French, sash, studio, and bay windows, would put a halt to this malignant revolution: the writer would be constrained to use the available properties on the premises or take his play to another theatre.

The disorganized poverty of designers in former years has at last been organized. They have banded together under the label "Scenic Artists' Union," and managed to enforce a closed shop agreement with the producers which practically guarantees full unemployment to ninety per cent of the membership.

There are, at present count, three hundred and twenty-five members in the union who are qualified to design sets and costumes. This figure excludes the one hundred and twenty-five costume designers and a strange huddle of fifty specialists corralled together under the clinical legend "The Diorama Group." Of the aforementioned three hundred and twenty-five, only twenty-five to thirty will normally be employed in a season; of these, only eight or nine will design more than one show a year; of these, only two or three will do more than half of the sixty to seventy productions put on in an average year.

These figures, cheerfully given out by the union, have in no way discouraged aspiring designers from trying to crash this exclusive, unemployed set. The past year one hundred and twenty-five applications for membership were received and seventeen new members were grudgingly accepted. The union has tried desperately but unsuccessfully to persuade these lemmings from joining their unhappy ranks.

You, as a prospective applicant, will be forewarned that even though you should pass the technical and financial requirements imposed by the union, you must then submit yourself for unanimous approval to the general membership, in secret ballot. Escaping the pox of a blackball dropped by a loving fellow-artist, you then—and then only—have the legal right to be unemployed in the theatre. This well-earned distinction of "full-fledged member" also carries with it the threat of oblivion.

Further benefits to be derived from your membership are as follows: You may now enter any theatre in the United States by merely presenting your union card to the box-office treasurer along with the price of the ticket, in cash. There also will be paid to your estate a fraternal cash reward of five hundred dollars when you drop dead.

7

ANGEL AUDITIONS

THE FIRST and most important of all auditions is the angel audition.

An angel is a man or woman with money eager to invest in a play or musical in the hopes of making more money.

A "Sorry, old man" from an important angel after an audition is more disastrous than a "Good God, what happened last night" review from Brooks Atkinson the morning after an opening night.

An approving nod accompanied by a check from a celebrated angel acts as a catalyst on the other, less demonstrative angels. A wondrous thing to behold. For unless this strange alchemy takes place there will never be a show.

Angel auditions are held in borrowed apartments and private homes. The general procedure is to equip each of the thirty or forty angels with a Scotch-and-soda and seat them informally about the room. The producer then steps forward and introduces himself in stuttered prose. He admits modestly of his general business acumen, his frugality, his honesty, his ability to recognize a good script when he sees one, confessing he doesn't know a damn thing about Art. This last statement is sure-fire. The angels know they are in safe hands.

On one of these occasions it was my unpleasant duty to be present as co-author of an impending musical. My collaborator in this heinous crime was S. J. Perelman, who shall always be remembered for penning the immortal line, "I've got Bright's disease and he's got mine."

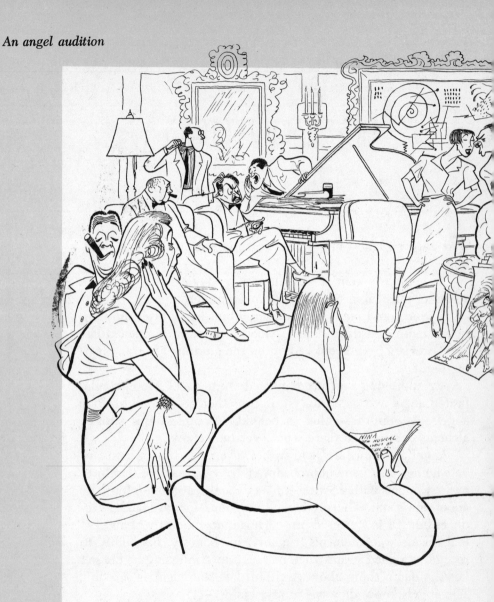

Our producer, having completed his own dossier, then dis-
closed the title of our musical, *Sweet Bye and Bye*. (Little did
anyone suspect the calamitous destinies chalked up for us. Before we had finished with rehearsals, two members of our com-

pany wound up in laughing academies unable to remember their own names; another took to drink; our director has since become a successful actor; we wore out four producers before we finally opened in New Haven; Perelman and I were forced to leave the country; and three hundred thousand dollars was eventually spent on the burial of *Sweet Bye and Bye* when it died the night of September 21, 1946, at the Erlanger Theatre in Philadelphia.)

The room that night was full of trusting, optimistic, smiling faces. They were great; our producer was great; we were great; it was a great big wonderful world.

In response to the thunderous applause (which carried clear across the room) at the mere mention of our names, Perelman and I, equipped with the symbols of our respective crafts— sheep dog, pipe and tweeds, and smock, Windsor tie, and beard —rose to acknowledge this ovation by politely bowing, first to the assembled guests and then to each other. To this very day I carry on the top of my skull a wen, about the size of a robin's egg, where our heads met on that memorable evening.

The other defendants—lyricist Ogden Nash, composer Vernon Duke, designer Boris Aronson, choreographer Fred Kelly— were each introduced in turn with short obituaries.

The ritual differed in no way, except for personnel, from

the many other auditions being held in similarly borrowed apartments throughout the city. No doubt at this very moment there are angels sprinkling cigar ashes on appropriated carpets, stuffing half-eaten sandwiches in the crevices of other people's upholstered furniture, pouring unpalatable drinks in the potted rubber plants of strangers, while a brave little band of troupers performs and bows for its supper.

The introductions finally dispensed with, it is now the producer's job to captivate and charm his audience. This mesmerization is usually achieved by delivering an illiterate synopsis of the book muttered between clenched teeth and finishing all sentences with the question, "You see?" Extraneous wry comments and chain smoking, interspersed with rapid shots of straight bourbon, also help to create an excellent impression. The angel, accustomed to these unintelligible proceedings, will be impressed with the showmanship of the affair.

An exodus to the kitchen or bar is called for after the reading—the producer amiably suggesting they discuss quite freely their honest feeling about the book. The author, anxious to know how his book went over, cannot restrain himself from eavesdropping on these discussions. I can report, with some authority, nothing happens.

Fit subjects for conversation during these debate periods are confined to the stock market, the weather, off-color jokes, anecdotes about you and Rockefeller, the situation abroad, dieting, and the "By God, I've never seen you looking better" routine.

The audition continues after the mellowed angels are eventually reseated. It is now the composer's and lyricist's show. They take over from the producer by launching into a sprightly rendition of the opening song; this is a bounce-sock number which will stop the show. Next comes a catchy rhythm number with tricky lyrics which definitely is a show stopper. As a matter of fact, from the time our hero describes himself musically, in the opening scene of the book, as a schmendrick with a noodle for a brain, up until the first-act finale where he breaks with the girl because she indiscreetly allowed herself to be photographed as "the pin-down girl of the year," every song is a show stopper. And "I Love You" and "Darling, I Love You" are touted as the two numbers destined for the Hit Parade. The composer carefully explains why he put the two Hit Parade tunes in the first act. It seems that during the intermission immediately following it is advantageous to get your audience whistling and singing these tunes up and down the street in front of the theatre. This sage observation never fails to get a "These fellows really know their business all right" look of approbation from the beatific angels.

The reconciliation of the lovers, after the opening ballet of the second act, is followed by two newsboys running back and forth across the stage shouting the headlines of the day. This device, calculated to divert and entertain the audience for the next twenty minutes (this could conceivably be cut to eighteen minutes; it is always difficult at this stage of the show to estimate accurately), gives the stage crew time to set up the big finale scene backstage. This technique of stage craft is known as a "dissolve" (the movies use the same trick) and allows one scene to flow into the next one, continuous and uninterrupted, except for the newsboys running back and forth across the stage shouting the headlines of the day.

After the "dissolve," the solid gold curtain is raised exposing the breath-taking finale. Perched on a crescent moon, high above a revolving penthouse, we discover our hero and his bride, deep in an embrace, singing another show-stopping melody, "Sweetheart, I Love You."

The innovation of placing this Hit Parade tune in the finale is a daring (the word "revolutionary" is considered in bad taste at angel auditions) departure from the conventional row of girls and principals singing to the audience, "We think you're swell." The composer reassures everyone that, based on his experience, it is advisable to send the audience out into the night whistling and singing his finale song in taxis, subways, and bars after the show.

A smattering of applause, indicative of nothing at all and never varying in intensity from one audition to another, brings the audition to a close. Everybody shakes everybody else's hand and then with a few last words from the producer, destined to destroy whatever esprit the musical performance engendered, the angels depart, each bearing a mimeographed copy of the budget.

These budgets meticulously account for every shoe, stock-

The angels depart

ing, paper clip, rubber band, electric bulb, flat, prop, and stick of furniture, railroad fare, typed manuscript, toilet paper, and photo frame. The fees for lawyers, scenic designer, costume designer, director, press agent, general manager, company manager, stage manager, stage crew, electricians, wardrobe mistresses, musicians, the cast, and a strange man listed as "procurer of materials." Carefully listed down to the last penny are the authors' royalties, theatre rentals, rehearsal halls, hauling charges, insurance, printing, taxes, office rent, and miscellaneous. Also included are the deposits required by Actors' Equity and Local 802, the Musicians' Union, and A.T.A.M., the press agents' and managers' union, and I.A.T.S.E., the stagehands' union.

The cherry on top of this formidable recipe is referred to on the budget as "Probable out-of-town losses." Watch out for this one! It's a lethal item. For there is no accurate way of estimating this premeditated reality. The usual custom is to put down an arbitrary figure to round out the budget so that the total will end with zeros. As an example: The actual production costs tally $273,489.66; your assumed out-of-town losses would then be $26,510.34, making a handy, convenient total of $300,000.00 to play around with.

All I can say, with painfully clear reminiscence, is that when a production is in trouble and desperately needs major fixing, there is not enough money in Fort Knox to see it through.

Employing dybbuks, blackmail, guile, cock-eyed luck, and thirty or forty auditions, the angels are eventually persuaded to part with their money. The collecting and spending of this money is what we mean when we speak of the "legitimate" theatre of today. The experimental theatres, or off-Broadway theatres, by way of contrast, are financed by culture-crazy angels who also buy paintings from living artists. The experimental-theatre angel wears his hair long or shaves it all off but never gets a haircut.

8

AUDITIONS FOR ACTORS

THE THEATRE is the only business in the world where prospective employees are made to sing, dance, recite, and parade in their underwear before they are hired. It makes no difference whether you are an experienced actor or an unemployed Fudgicle salesman—if you want to act, you must audition.

A really first-rate actor or actress can sense an audition before it has been scheduled. Across the years these professionals have developed an anticipatory sense similar to the vultures of northern Siam. (On a recent journey of mine to this remote land, I was told by the natives that the vulture during the last war would ominously appear over a village hours before it was actually bombed.)

Second-rate professionals, drifters, disillusioned housewives, stage-struck screwballs, pupils of unemployed actors, and all those who can't sleep at night will be alerted by some mysterious and incalculable underground system. No one has ever inserted a want ad for actors in our daily press. Nevertheless, drama schools, agents' offices, Actors' Equity, Broadway restaurants, Pina-Cola stands, furnished rooming houses, Park Avenue penthouses, Drive-ins, Walgreens, and the Astor Drugstore will be emptied of aspiring Thespians on audition day. Another strange phenomenon is the long-distance call from an unknown relative pleading, "Would it hurt you to give the boy a chance?"

To forestall fainting actresses on doorsteps, and stage-struck waitresses reciting *Camille* during lunch, and breach-of-promise suits, and attempted rape charges, it is prudent to announce publicly the time and date of contemplated auditions. The drama columns, the agents, and the actors themselves will respond to this humane treatment with amazing alacrity.

It is well to remember that no secret is ever kept on Broadway. Sam Zolotow, of the New York *Times,* will ferret your latent plans before they are conceived, and *Show Business,* a weekly guide published by Leo Shull, dedicates itself to the exposure of unlisted private telephone numbers, home addresses of active producers, playwrights, and directors, their favored haunts, and the most likely time they may be reached at any hour of the day or night. A clandestine deal consummated in your own soundproof study in Erwinna, Pennsylvania, will be reported, word for word, in the next day's drama columns.

The activities and whereabouts of potential investors are covered in another publication titled *Angels, Inc.* This annual is also published by the aforementioned Leo Shull.

The actor, either through the grapevine or the bold announcement, which I heartily recommend, will, in any case, be apprised of the audition. He looks forward to this day with childlike ecstasy, knowing full well that it will be the most harrowing day in his professional life. A first audition for an actor (assuming that he has already served his apprenticeship in the arts by painting barns for a bankrupt theatre producer in the summer, and imitated falling apples in some accredited drama school in the winter) should be arranged through an agent. The usual procedure—after the actor has filed his name, address, phone number, and physical description with every agent in the city—is to make a daily call in person or by phone and inquire, "What goes?" The day inevitably arrives when the agent knows of a part which fits the actor like an old glove, and it usually is just about as interesting. The play is a one-set, living-room drama, sort of experimental; it has no fireplace. The part calls for an actor aged twenty-two and a half, blond, 5′ 11″ tall, English accent, must have wart on right hand and a limp in left leg. With the exception of the limp, the description fits our actor perfectly.

An audition appointment is made with the director, and on the fateful day we discover our actor limping out of his fur-

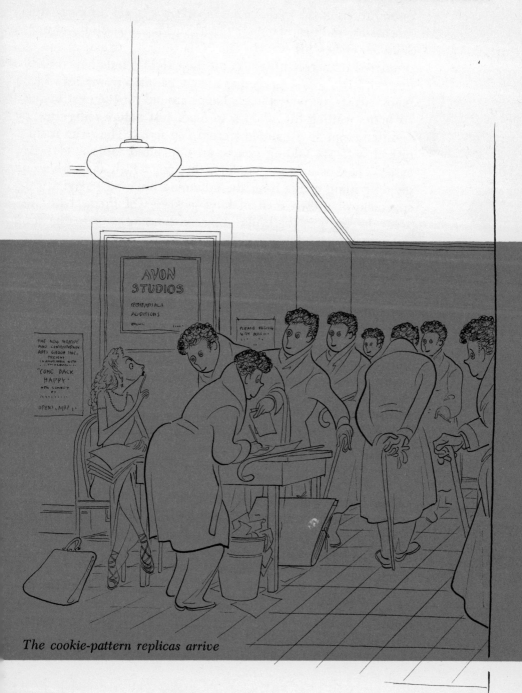

The cookie-pattern replicas arrive

nished room in the mid-Forties, sporting a turtle-neck sweater, moccasins, and his roommate's suit. Sucking a mouthful of Sen-Sens, he makes his way to the Nola Studios, where a line of simulated limpers with warts on their right hands has already formed. Visibly discouraged at the cookie-pattern replica of his fellow-artists, he nevertheless hangs around for the next five or six hours waiting for his turn to read. Just before entering the audition room he is handed a crumpled script. The room is furnished with six folding chairs, an unpainted table, and brief cases. There is a large window, through which may be seen giggling filing clerks from the adjoining building enjoying the spectacle of grown men making jackasses of themselves. An actor, having just read, may be seen limping over to the unpainted table, where he will leave his name and address. A loud argument is taking place between the producer and his stage manager over "a piece of business." The director, engrossed in a letter from a former girl friend who threatens to expose him unless she gets a part in the show (the fact that it is an all-male cast is irrelevant to her), looks up from his correspondence, examines minutely the wart on our actor's right hand, has him limp around the room a few times while he rereads his mail, finally rises, and, satisfied with the cursory inventory, explains the part to our actor. "Your mother and father died when you were three years old. You have taken this job as butler for the Von Morzer Bruyns to pay your tuition in an advanced atomic correspondence course. Now, none of this, of course, ever comes out in the play, but I just want to acquaint you with the 'feel' of the character. . . . Y'understand?" Patting our actor lightly on the head to make him feel at ease, and at the same time assuring himself that the actor is not wearing a wig, he continues: "Okay, son. Go ahead. Read!" The barely legible script, hardly improved by the mass handling, is now deciphered by our actor, who, by this time, is an exposed nerve. "By God, Herman—if it's the last thing I do—I'll never—" He is interrupted by the director. "Thank you very much. Will you be good enough to leave your name and address with the girl on your way out?" Signaling his assistant, he calls out, "Next, please!"

Our actor, thoroughly discouraged by his first audition, gives

The audition

up the theatre for more lucrative fields, settling for a job as a professional model. His agent meanwhile has been combing the city for him. After days of frantic search, the agent finally locates him lying around on the floor of some photographer's studio. Our actor is handed a contract for the part for which he auditioned. Years later, on the edge of a swimming pool in Bel-Air, with the fragrance of hibiscus, jasmine, dying wolfhounds, and steam laundries permeating the air, our actor, reminded of these early struggles in his career, will have you thrown out. That's the theatre for you.

Musical auditions are usually held in rented theatres, the dancers in one and the singers in another. The dancers are brought on stage in groups of twenty. In bathing suits and underwear, holding their street clothes and pocketbooks over their arms, they parade before the dance director and his as-

56

sistants and a couple of other fellows who just like to see undressed women. Girls not conforming to height, color, and
width are immediately eliminated. The remaining nine are
asked: "How many of you can do a split? Raise your hands,
please." All hands are raised. "How many can do a jumping
split from a table?" All but two raise their hands. The seven
girls are then lined up and one by one they jump from the
table, defying gravity and sanity, in a perfect split onto the
stage floor. Their names are taken by the stage manager as a
new group of twenty girls, fastening themselves, are ushered on
stage. These tests are continued for the rest of the day, at the
end of which the dance director has a list of a hundred and fifty
girls, all about the same height and width, who can jump from
a table in a split. More elimination tests, involving tap rou-
tines, acrobatics, ballet, and contortion, are held until at last

the required six dancers are hired at minimum Equity rates.

Everybody keeps his clothes on at the singing auditions. A male or female singer, accompanied by his respective singing teacher, is led on stage. The accompanist carries a brief case loaded with "professional copies" of every song published in the twentieth century. The director from out front, sensing danger, bellows: "Listen, sweetheart—one song—that's all we've got time for." A hurried conference between the Svengali and his pupil and a selection is decided upon. If the singer is a girl it usually is "Chiri-Biri-Bean." The boys invariably choose "On the Road

The singers' audition

to Mandalay." After six or seven hours of this it becomes increasingly difficult to distinguish voices and sexes. It is not uncommon during these trials to have a voice coach applaud his Trilby after a "Chiri-Biri-Bean" rendition and demand an encore. It is on these infrequent occasions that a hefty stage manager becomes a valuable asset to any company. The director, composer, and lyricist, after days of auditioning torch singers, folk singers, opera singers, hot, cold, and blue singers, crooners, stylists, Be-bop, and those with special material, settle for a chorus of untalented pretty girls.

9

REHEARSALS

MOST REHEARSALS are held in darkened theatres with an exposed thousand-watt electric light bulb illuminating the center of the stage. I have consulted many directors, actors, and lighting experts in an effort to find out why this naked bulb (producing migraine and temporary blindness) is essential during rehearsals. Everyone agrees that a protecting shade over the bulb would be a distinct advance, but the prejudice of tradition is a tough thing to overcome, particularly in the theatre. It took many years before the asbestos curtain was accepted. This humane curtain, designed to prevent burning actors from setting fire to the audience, eventually has become stock equipment in every theatre in the land. The simultaneous cremation of the actor and the audience has finally become a thing of the past. Progress in the theatre is slow.

The "pilot light" accounts for the many actors one sees hobbling along Broadway with the aid of crutches and smoked glasses. Members of the cast herded on stage under this obsolete beacon are made to walk a plank in pitch darkness to the auditorium floor. This ramp, cleverly designed without hand railings, is the supreme test. Surviving members are then taken to the men's room, where the rehearsals are continued.

It is mandatory for the director to wear a "Reinhardt cape" at all rehearsals. This cape is an ordinary overcoat thrown loosely over the shoulders, with the empty sleeves left dangling. (The cape derives its name from the late German director who gave everyone his first chance in the theatre, with the notable

*The prejudice of tradition is a tough thing
to overcome*

exception of Stanislavsky, who gave everyone his first chance in the theatre.) A really first-rate director has an assistant who keeps retrieving the falling coat from spittoons, sandboxes, and careless actors trampling on it.

The playwright during rehearsals is seated out front with a smoldering Lily cup full of dying cigarette butts. One can always spot an inexperienced playwright by the holes burned in his pants during rehearsal. These folk are also easily upset by a wrong reading of their lines, such as "I could see her behind all of it" into "I could see her behind—all of it."

Cooling systems and heating plants remain hermetically sealed during the rehearsal period. Fainting spells and pneumonia are common occupational hazards of the theatre. No actor worth his salt is in fit condition opening night. The exaltation of overcoming laryngitis or a hacking cough as the curtain rises on opening night symbolizes, if further proof were needed, man's triumph over the bug.

The producer, director, stage manager, and doorman are treated as gods for the first five days of rehearsal. Their slightest whim is eagerly satisfied. Members of the cast are constantly embracing each other. They know it is considered unprofes-

sional to applaud during rehearsal, but they cannot restrain themselves from gasping, laughing, weeping, and sighing at each other's performance. This camaraderie disappears completely on the sixth day of rehearsal. This is the day they step on the director's cape, order the producer out of the theatre, send the stage manager out for sandwiches and coffee, and fight for the best dressing room. No more licking each other from ear to ear; no more hearty greetings of "darling," "sweetheart." All these amenities come abruptly to a halt on the sixth day. The death watch has been completed. For on this day of rehearsal the fate of the actors' employment no longer rests with the management. To fire an actor after the five-day test period requires impeachment proceedings.

Toupées, fingernail polish, costume jewelry, stockings, clean shirts, and capped teeth disappear on this day. Beards and eyebrows are allowed to flourish for the remaining three weeks of rehearsal.

Actors are allowed to move chairs and tables during rehearsals. These are not considered props. A lamp, however, is a prop. Unlit, this lamp may be handled by only one man, the property man. Lit, it requires two men to put it in place—the electrician and the property man. This ritual maintains the actor's dignity and at the same time employs two men in their chosen professions.

Last-minute changes, producer's suggestions, director's blue pencilings, financial estimates, and whisky and gravy stains having obliterated all other scripts extant, the stage manager remains the sole member of the company with a whole legible script. With the script zealously guarded, he stations himself at stage right (which naturally is on the left side of the stage) and prompts the floundering performers in their lines, cues, and positions.

There is hardly an actor alive who can restrain himself from tampering with the line given him by the playwright. This improvement is called "padding." If the playwright is adamant, insisting the actor recite his line exactly as it was written, the actor will slur the reading. The garbled reading of the line is called "throwing it away." The "padding" and "throwing it away" are constant problems to be adjusted during rehearsals. As an example: An actor, with the stage all to himself, has the line "Come in." This line, he feels, "has nothing in it . . . it's not comfortable in the mouth." The obvious and inevitable consequence of "Come in" producing another actor through the door to share the stage with him is never voiced as an objection.

The actor, suddenly inspired, pleads with the director and playwright to let him interpret the line. These demands are usually acceded to, for the alternative is to have the line "thrown away." The company stands by while the actor works out his interpretation of the line "Come in."

Alone on the stage, his thoughts spoken aloud (a little to himself and mostly to the audience), he speculates, "That must be George at the door." Extracting from space an imagined twenty-year-old armagnac, he proceeds to pour himself a drink. Fondling and inhaling from the unseen glass, he raises it aloft, heroically toasting his unknown past; then, suddenly, with great violence, he smashes the invisible glass in the nonexistent fireplace. An unborn wail dies in his throat as he regains his composure. Carefully selecting, out of the air, a book about the size of *Simplicissimus,* he lights his pipe, settles himself on the divan, and says, "Come in, George!"

Two hours and six cups of coffee after this charade, a compromise is effected whereby the actor is allowed to add "George" to the original line "Come in," on condition all other business is eliminated. The actor is content with his padding and the line will not be thrown away. The winning or losing of these exasperating battles during rehearsals determines your staying power in the theatre.

When the actors have learned their sides (a side is the individual player's part typed on a small piece of paper. This device enables the actor to play his part without knowing what the rest of the play is about), they are put on their feet and directed in movement. It is not uncommon, at rehearsal, to witness an actress fondly caressing an imagined child in her arms, moan like a wounded coyote, crawl around the dirty stage on her hands and knees, pleading forgiveness from a hat rack; or to see a lone actor practice the removal of a visiting card from his wallet and extend it to a brick wall, mumbling his lines over and over again to himself; or to hear, simultaneously, a maniacal laugh emanate from an off-stage dressing room, as audible testimony of another actor hard at work. When all these bits of business are reasonably perfected, the players are then ready for a dress rehearsal.

Performers at a dress rehearsal are usually enraptured with their colleagues' costumes and disenchanted with their own.

Ordinary human beings walking around on stage (seen from out front mingling with the players who are in full make-up and costume) seem, by contrast, inhumanly grotesque. They all look mildewed. Even the chi-chi *couturière*, who up to that moment was an attractive personality, suddenly appears as a harridan with a face full of pins and a figure resembling a bundle of dirty wash tied in the middle. The director, an ordinary citizen in Lindy's, when seen standing next to the leading lady with her beaded lashes, invented mouth, calligraphed eyebrows, and Nu-skin, looks like a sand hog with an anvil for a behind. One is immediately aware of the badly drawn nude tattooed on the stage manager's bared arm, and the producer's hitherto vivacious secretary stands like simulated taxidermy alongside these beautiful people.

The crises of the leading lady refusing to appear in the three-thousand-dollar gown especially designed for her, the male star insisting he would never have signed with this crumby management had he known what he was letting himself in for, the other members of the cast complaining the buttons are too big for the buttonholes, the zippers gratuitously nip off pieces of loose flesh, the bloomers are too tight for dancing, the shoes pinch, the electric canes don't light, the angel wings dig holes in their backs, and the strapless evening gowns won't stay up— all these normal disasters are met by the experienced designer with great calm. On one occasion I was spectator at a dress rehearsal when the designer, in front of the entire company, accused her assistant of being the culprit responsible for the ill-fitting costumes and summarily fired her. The actors, chagrined at the sight of anyone being fired for any reason, took up the cudgels in defense of the assistant. It took all their combined persuasive petitions to wheedle a reprieve for the unfortunate helper. The buttons, the zippers, the bloomers, the shoes, the canes, the wings, and the denuding gowns were forgotten in the emotional scene.

After the dress rehearsal a run-through of the complete show takes place. The run-through is usually held the day be-

Performers are usually enraptured with their colleagues'

costumes and disenchanted with their own

fore the out-of-town opening. "Experts" and friends are called in to witness the proceedings and advise from an audience point of view. At a run-through of Saroyan's *Hello Out There* which I attended, I discovered a strange group of "experts" seated in the auditorium. Saroyan had chosen these "experts" with great care. There were five of them—Joe Gould, writer, whose *Oral History* is one of the largest unpublished manuscripts in the history of literature; Max Bodenheim, poet and indestructible bohemian; Clarinet Pete, strolling minstrel, who plays two clarinets at the same time along Sixth Avenue in the Forties; Bill Cody, sidewalk chalk artist, who looks and dresses like Buffalo Bill; and a fellow by the name of Zvoboda.

After the performance, Saroyan went over to Bill Cody and inquired, "Well, Bill, how did you like the play?" Cody, visibly moved, with tears streaming through his beard, said, "It's the greatest goddamned show I ever saw." Saroyan then asked, "Tell me, Bill, did you ever see a play before?" and Cody replied, "Nope—first show I ever saw."

During these turbulent days without sun, the press agent occasionally sneaks around the darkened house with a photographer and artist in tow. The management, the cast, and the director know these strangers are groping their way through impenetrable shadows out front. As a matter of fact, they pay the press agent a handsome weekly fee for his services, but they pretend he and his comrades are not there until their assignments are finished. Then all hell breaks loose. "How can anyone rehearse with all those damn flash bulbs going off?"—"Who gave you permission to break in here?"—"What is this? A theatre or a circus?"—"Out, out! All of you. And that goes for you, too. You, over there with the beard. Out. Get the hell out of here and let's get to work!"

The press agent, the photographer, and the artist all play the game in dead seriousness. Deposited on the sidewalk in front of the theatre in blinding daylight, the trio, accustomed to the enveloping darkness of the theatre, retreat to the nearest bar, where not a word of these strange rites is ever mentioned.

10

OUT-OF-TOWN OPENING

MOST BROADWAY productions preview their wares in New Haven, Boston, Philadelphia, Wilmington, or Baltimore to get away from the Broadway crowd of "experts."

Most Broadway "experts" go to New Haven, Boston, Philadelphia, Wilmington, or Baltimore to see the out-of-town opening.

As the curtain rises on your production in, say, New Haven, and you find yourself standing in the back of the crowded house scanning the audience, you cannot help but feel proud of your accomplishment—of a job well done. Make the most of this short-lived euphoria, for impending disaster awaits you. At that very moment, the costumes for the opening number are being unloaded at the stage door. With the curtain up, exposing some of the actors in street clothes and the others in costume, you are well on your way to your first ulcer. As the show progresses, various props belatedly arrive. Electrical effects that worked perfectly a half hour before curtain time suddenly blow a fuse and belch forth a streak of blue lightning, incapacitating the stage manager, who is the only one who knows all the light cues for the rest of the show. These minor catastrophes, unnoticed by the spectators out front, create bedlam backstage. Actors who were letter perfect during rehearsals become confused on stage and exit through the fireplace instead of the door. The baton flies out of the conductor's hand during the overture and is caught by an eccentric patron who refuses to return it. The audience co-operates by obliterating all sounds emanating from the stage; they perform by waving to old friends whom they haven't seen since dinner. They cough, wheeze, sniffle, sneeze, talk, hiccup, and set fire to their programs in an effort to read them by match light. (The information in the program, apart from the misspelling of actors' names, is based on the original script and bears not the slightest resemblance to the reshuffled scenes depicted on the stage.)

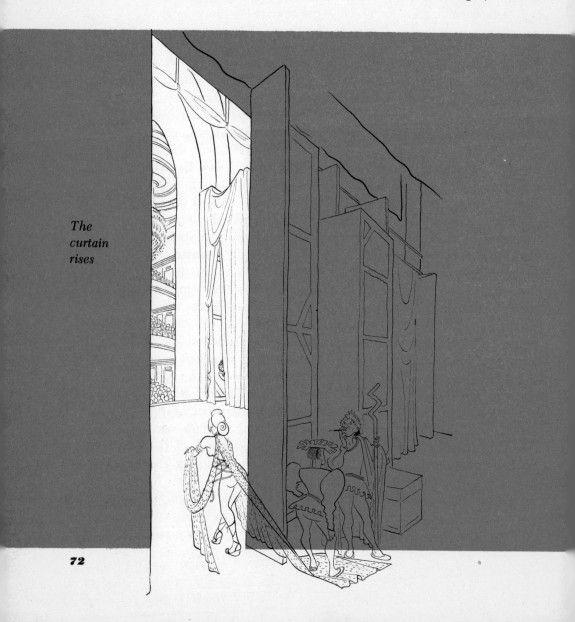

The curtain rises

Hollywood agents, talent scouts, angels, rival producers who previously had rejected the script, actors' agents, authors' agents, music agents, dance agents, and free-lance agents, as well as relatives and old friends, will all be there with knives for your New Haven opening.

After the performance wakes are held in hotel rooms, bars, dressing rooms, and coffee shops. Every hair of the production is pulled out with a fine comb. The players are told how to improve their make-up and their performance. The authors are given bits of paper with whole scenes rewritten on them. You are advised that unless you abandon the project Forty-sixth Street will laugh at you. Well-meaning friends will leave no doubt in the lyricist's mind that he has written some wonderful unsingable lyrics. The composer and designer usually are the heroes at these midnight sessions; they are made to feel they have pooled their talents with a bunch of quacks.

Others feel it their duty to rush to the nearest phone and report the glad tidings, via long distance, to the New York drama editors. "A course, it's only a tryout, y'understand—but I'm tellin' ya, it's a real toikey. Yeah. . . . S'too bad. . . . An' the tough part is, the kids are friends a mine what wrote it. . . . I was rootin' for 'em, see? All the way. But what can y'do? If it ain't there, it ain't there. Yeah, yeah. Don't mention it. Be seein' ya."

Twenty-four hours after your New Haven opening you are a dead duck in New York. Nothing is printed in the New York daily press (most drama editors pay no attention to the general hysteria you have wrought in the theatre world), but actors rejected at your earlier auditions will now be toasting your flop with unrestrained revelry. The Shuberts are worried about the booking they promised you. Mr. Sardi speculatively scans the pile of unpaid chits you had signed during rehearsals. The angels who didn't invest in your enterprise will be smugly congratulating each other on their shrewd acumen in spotting a stinker.

It is necessary for you to wait until the following Wednesday for the weekly *Variety* to appear with a professional estimate of your chances for survival. This bible of show business (to coin a phrase) will inform you that your show "needs fixing." That it has "a weak second act," although the "basic idea is good." To sum it up: "It has about as much chance as a Chinese concessionaire in Japan." However, "If they can get this one moving smoothly, should be strictly in the 'hit' department." In short, there is nothing that could possibly happen to you, here or in the hereafter, which *Variety*'s haruspex will not have divined for you in advance. Every contingency will be taken care of, except your ulcers and a demoralized cast.

With all the evidence in, you follow the sage advice of friends and experts and hire a "play doctor" after the Saturday night performance in New Haven.

The play doctor—closeted in a suite at the Warwick Hotel in Philadelphia, with an unlimited supply of benzedrine, coffee,

and corned beef, industriously working away punching gags and business in the script—emerges, a broken man after forty-eight hours, with freshly typed sides for the cast to insert in that evening's performance. No one connected with the production knows of his existence. You have been saving this surprise as a sort of shot in the arm to a rapidly disintegrating cast.

The original authors, having given their tacit approval to any script changes (by taking to the hills after the New Haven opening), are no longer a source of irritation to you. With the writers out of the way, you are deluded into thinking yourself complete arbiter of the public taste.

Early Monday morning, with the official opening scheduled for that night in Philadelphia, you assemble the entire company on stage. The play doctor, groggy and a bit shorter than when you last saw him (he has worn his legs into his belly pacing up and down his suite at the Warwick for the past two days), is introduced to the ensemble. Cries of "Hear, hear!" from the cast bring a suggestion of moisture to your weasel eyes. With a "This is it!" assurance, you hand the edited manuscript to your director as you would a mink coat to a blonde.

Your surprise will be genuine when the director, after a cursory reading of the new material, realizing that he is supposed to restage practically the whole play before the evening performance, carefully rolls the script into a tight bat and tries to open your skull with it. This attempted mayhem carries with it a running commentary by the director on your general qualifications as a producer.

The Broadway mob, always suspicious of cast changes, fixing, or improvement on the road, will be genuinely alarmed when they discover your director has thrown in the towel. The press agent, at this point, is usually called in to save the day. Through a carefully worded release to the press, he explains how your director, through an unavoidable accident, opened a vein in his arm while trying to start his car in a hermetically sealed garage.

Needless to say, there is not enough time to insert the contemplated revisions before the evening performance, and besides, you are now without a director. If you stubbornly insist on opening, it will play pretty much the same as it did in New Haven. Nothing will have been gained by going on the road. A hurried conference with your business manager, press agent, and other advisers will make you see the wisdom of postponing the opening until the following Monday. New ads, press releases, and cocktail parties are frantically prepared for Philadelphia.

A hurried conference

The play doctor, with a guaranteed percentage of the gross, is finally persuaded to take over the direction. He has only one week to whip the production into shape. He utilizes these precious days by moving the sofa from one side of the stage to the other, changing the ring of the doorbell to a chime, replacing the ex-director's girl friend with his own niece in a minor part, allowing himself to be interviewed by video, radio, the press, and high-school and trade publications. With the public conscience appeased, and your advance sales in New York dwindling to less than the weekly salary of the box-office treasurer, you are at long last ready for your Philadelphia opening.

Unfortunately, the first-string Philadelphia reviewers will not be able to cover your opening. Once having forfeited your original opening date, you must now pay the price. You neglected to check, before announcing your new opening date, whether there was any other opening scheduled for that night. There usually is. Your fate now rests in the hands of the second-string reviewers, recruited from the sports department of the local dailies. There is nothing your press agent or anybody else can do about this. A "Why didn't somebody tell me about this?" will avail you nothing. You can either postpone the opening again (this choice will make loyal enemies of all the sports writers in Philadelphia, who next year may be covering the drama as their regular stint) or open as scheduled and take your lumps like a nice guy.

After all, *Oklahoma!*, the greatest money-making musical of all time, suffered a similar fate on the road. Howard Cullman, celebrated angel, refused to invest in it after seeing it performed in New Haven. Billy Rose turned thumbs down on it, and Mike Todd said, "*Oklahoma!* is not commercial."

Remember *The Heiress*. It opened in Boston and was unmercifully battered by the critics and audience. Oscar Serlin, producer of *Life with Father*, was the producer of *The Heiress*. He gave it an expert production, managed to get John Halliday out of retirement in Honolulu to play the leading part, and everyone agreed that the play, written by Ruth and Augustus Goetz, just wasn't up to the audience's discriminating taste. Jed Harris, for no sane reason, bought the play after it had folded in Boston and reproduced it some months later in New York, where it developed into a smash hit. Ruth and Augustus Goetz, who had a tough time getting up the room rent after the Boston closing of *The Heiress,* now employ a special tax consultant to straighten out their income taxes, and when I last heard from them they were working in Hollywood, where they lived in a house with a swimming pool on the second floor.

Then there were Gallagher and Shean, who, after playing twelve consecutive weeks to enthusiastic audiences in the Palace Theatre on Broadway, were booed off the stage the following week in Philadelphia.

The enigmatic fates of others, too numerous to mention, since practically every show opening on the road is a saga unto itself, will bolster your flagging optimism.

What with hauling charges, railroad fares, full salaries, staggering costs of music rehearsals with a new pit orchestra (a union must) in each town, and the advertising and publicity attending an out-of-town opening, you may very well question whether all these expenses are worth the dubious romances consummated on the road. It seems a stiff price to pay for the privilege of getting away from your wife for a couple of weeks.

Apart from insomnia and a few cases of coffee poisoning, nothing much is accomplished on the road tryout except the opportunity it affords the boys of the ensemble to make up their minds whether they are A.C., or D.C., or A.C.-D.C.

11

NEW YORK OPENING

PRACTICALLY EVERYONE attending an opening night in New York has some special reason for being there, with the notable exception of Mr. Ira and Mrs. Rita Katzenberg and Hope Hampton. The Katzenbergs (retired shoe people) and Miss Hampton (retired movie queen) buy their opening-night tickets—always in the first row—and merely watch the performance, as ordinary people do every other night in the year.

Most important openings take place during the winter and spring because of the blizzards and rain common during these seasons in New York. Opening-night weather is so calculated that the first-nighter, in his frantic search for an empty taxi, will, in most cases, arrive late for the performance.

The crowded outer lobby of the theatre is permeated with a unique redolence. A potpourri of the perfumery of perfumes blended with rain-soaked mink, sweet-scented bath salts, wet new leather, ambrosial hair oils, garlic, pungent Martinis, damp corsages, boutonnieres, and witch hazel. The social importance of the event coincides with the quality of the aroma. The potency of the scent (similar to incense and candles in other temples of worship) has a decidedly intoxicating effect on your senses. You are elated. You are excited. You feel younger, as if you have just washed your feet.

The producer, the angels, the relatives, the director, and the performers are each endowed with a different and personal kind of hysterics before the curtain is raised on your creation. Restrain yourself from yelling "Stop!" as the curtain goes up because you have at that precise moment thought of the perfect ending for the second act. It's too late. Your play, similar to your child, now has a life of its own. There is nothing more you can do about it. Any future cutting or polishing will be done on *you* and not on the play.

As you scan the solidly packed house of potential enemies, you may question your omnipotence as a playwright. In recent months you have become accustomed to having your slightest belch translated into a witty saying for nationally syndicated gossip columns. You are now faced with the likely prospect of reverting from an anecdote to a private citizen after tonight's exhibition. It was only last week that you changed your public telephone number to a private one, and now you find yourself looking around for a friendly face to say hello to. What happened? Why, nothing at all. Your analyst should have you up and around like a new man in a couple of years. A word of advice may be of inestimable value to you at this trying time. First of all, try not to think of the opportunity you neglected to take advantage of when the New York *Times* offered you space to write a Sunday article before the opening. Needless to say, had you explained in detailed prose to the critics and audience the obscure symbolism which you failed to clarify in your play, it could only have helped. But it's too late to brood over this lost chance now. Remember, you are still an unpublished genius, a celebrity, a potential man of distinction. Calvert may yet switch to you, and I assume you are still in your right mind. This right should now be immediately exercised by refusing to attend the party after the opening. These parties are held primarily for the purpose of embarrassing the playwright. If the notices delivered to the party hot off the presses are good, you will be ignored. The actors will thank their director, the director will thank his producer, the producer will thank his angels, and the angels will thank God. You will be left with a foolish grin on your face and no one to thank except your wife, who, in all probability, has left you long before the show got this far. If, however, the notices are bad, you and your irresponsible pen will be immediately recognized for what they are. There will be no doubt in anyone's mind as to the real culprit responsible for the unhappy plight of these good people who staked their reputations and fortunes on your miserable script. Experienced playwrights have learned to send congratulatory telegrams from distant climes.

The producer, enjoying his last supper at 21, is plied with drinks from well-meaning friends before the opening. Arriving at the theatre an hour before curtain, he weaves his way around backstage, licking all the actors and tripping over the cables. He eventually makes his way out to the front of the house, where he may be seen during the performance hiding behind a drape in an upper box, crawling up and down the aisles on his hands and knees whispering to angels, watching the reactions of the critics from a concealed hole in the ceiling, laughing it up with the standees in the back of the auditorium, eavesdropping on conversations during intermission, concluding his dizzy performance by screaming himself hoarse with shouts of "Bravo!" as the curtain descends.

The angels, with bits of caviar stuck on their chins, arrive after the opening curtain has been raised and unerringly step on all the drama critics as they grope their way to their seats. A "benefactor," having missed the drama critic's corn on his first try, will, on the pretext of retrieving a program, have another go at him on his way out. With the program held firmly in front of him like a stiletto, he dashes up and down the darkened aisle looking for the row his vacated seat is in. His friends audibly whisper, "Sss—sss! Over here—over here." Using his program for a seeing eye, he accidentally rips open the drama critic's fly as he apologetically wends his way back to his seat again. After a few minutes the comforting dark of the theatre and the droning words coming from the stage act as a soporific on him. His fluttering eyelids, visible testimony of will and lethargy fighting it out, finally submit to the inevitable and slowly seal themselves, hermetically blotting out his investment. With his head comfortably tucked in a stranger's fur coat, he snores through the first act. Rudely awakened by the bright house lights and general stampede signaling intermission, he rouses himself and seeks the nearest bar for a quick pick-me-up, returning to the theatre in time for the last half of the second act.

The relatives, with hacking coughs, are liberally sprinkled throughout the audience. These special pleaders, except for the unavoidable racket made while cracking walnuts and sucking

on peppermint canes during the performance, maintain a dignified silence. They sit stony-faced and unimpressed. Their monastic silence changes into demonstrative action when their boy makes his appearance on stage. They will beat their hands raw when their boy enters carrying a card tray, which he extends to the leading lady. His subsequent exit bearing the emptied card tray will also be accompanied by deafening applause by the relatives.

The director reassures every member of the cast separately that they are the greatest Thespians he has ever worked with and that he will personally see to it that they will never work again in the theatre if they fluff a line in their performance tonight.

The performers nervously wish each other success and gargle honey.

Armloads of telegrams from Hollywood and the Great Barrier Reef, flowers in baskets, boxes, and pots, gag newspapers printed with phony headlines, Worry birds, Shmoos, good-luck charms, and other tributes arrive backstage in an unending stream during the show. Never wish a European actor or actress good luck on opening night. Their prevailing superstitions demand that you tender your felicitations with disrespect, such as, "I hope you drop dead," or "Break your neck and legs."

There are those who insist that the balcony has a life of its own, that the future of the theatre lies up there. I have no way of accurately knowing about this. On the few occasions I have found myself on the shelf, it seemed to me that the audience was about the same as downstairs, except that the agents were sitting in the aisle seats instead of the drama critics.

Before the curtain is irretrievably raised, certain established rites are taking place backstage. Dancers, in last-minute attempts to break their backs, may be seen doing cartwheels, *entrechats*, elevations, spins, splits, and somersaults like demented grasshoppers on a parade ground. With the insistent clang of the warning bell, followed by a sharp rap on each dressing-room door from the perspiring stage manager screaming "Half hour!" all activities stop. Each performer, alone with butterflies fluttering around his insides, becomes a tower of superstition. Prayers are offered to neglected parents. Subconscious mumblings, like the humming of the insane, can be heard through the closed doors of dressing rooms.

Crucifixes, Mogen Davids, medallions, fetishes, phylacteries, horseshoes, wishbones, rabbit's feet, tephillin, elk's teeth, lucky pennies, amulets, and prayer wheels are employed to ward off the evil spirits. Twitching muscles, hitherto unknown, develop an irrepressible will of their own, and dance mad rigadoons just under the surface of the flesh. Saliva turns to kapok in the mouth. The booming voice of the stage manager announcing "Fifteen minutes" reacts on the novices like a sandbag dropped in a bowl of Jello. Even seasoned troupers fall apart during these last minutes before the long walk.

The musicians, unperturbed, finish their hand of pinochle and leisurely take their places in the pit. The cacophony of tuning instruments is abruptly silenced by the conductor, who sneaks in under the piano. His spotlighted appearance is the signal for the first applause of the evening. The applause itself is indicative of nothing at all. It merely serves as a sort of rehearsal for the audience to adjust the various cuppings of their hands to achieve the maximum amount of noise with the least amount of effort. These audience applause rehearsals will bear fruit later in the festivities. You will not be alone in your ignorance of the conductor's fame. No one knows who he is. After many years of theatregoing it may be possible to distinguish one conductor's bald head from another, but this is a field for the experts. To the average informed theatregoer these heads are as alike as plastics. The bright spotlight used to illumine the bald head also makes each piece of dandruff falling from this human salt shaker crystal clear to the furthest spectator.

The muted strains of the overture coming through backstage are drowned out by the stage manager bellowing his final warning, "On stage everybody! On stage everybody! On stage!" The assembled cast, some offering last-minute incantations, others desperately rehearsing their opening lines, are herded off stage behind the wings. A lone actor strumming a banjolele staggers into the blinding light on stage, and faces the vast impenetrable black of the auditorium. His plaintive tune, which

the director told him to hum very quietly in order to establish
the poetic mood necessary for the scene, becomes inaudible

over the burst of applause which greets the opening set. An electrical effect mysteriously explodes backstage. A grinning stagehand suddenly appears in the window of the set. A string snaps on the first violinist's fiddle. A gust of perfumed air sweeps the stage as the curtain rises, and gets stuck.

Some years ago, in Boston, I witnessed the opening of *Walk a Little Faster,* a musical with Beatrice Lillie and Bobby Clark, sponsored by one of our better producers, Courtney Burr. The opening curtain was raised on that memorable occasion and halfway up it got stuck. The brainless electrical device used for raising curtains persisted in its inexorable course until the curtain was torn loose from its moorings and with a resounding crash fluttered down over the musicians like a giant blanket. The entrapped musicians, under the mistaken impression that they were aboard a sinking clipper ship, continued their fiddling until a rescue was effected. (This show, incidentally, was written by Kiss-of-Death Perelman, Yip Harburg, Vernon Duke, and designed by Boris Aronson. It was also the first time any of these since famous theatre personalities had been employed in the theatre.)

Once the curtain is up, you are in that unenviable position of observing two years of work kaleidoscoped into a two-hour experience. Nothing said or seen will give you the slightest clue to your fate; the immediate, audible response of the audience will not in any way reflect their private opinions, so you might as well relax. First-night audiences seem equally as enchanted with a failure as with a success.

The City of New York employs special firemen backstage to see to it that the "No Smoking" edict is enforced. This ban is unofficially winked at on opening night, allowing the milling crowds of first-nighters, inextricably jammed in the halls and stairways after the performance, to singe each other with lighted cigarette butts. I once saw William Saroyan at the opening of his play *The Beautiful People* rush through the stage door of the Lyceum Theatre, accost the uniformed fireman stationed just inside, and pump his hand up and down. Saroyan congratulated the fireman on his wonderful performance under the confused, mistaken notion that he was talking to an actor.

The fireman modestly accepted the praise. It all seemed perfectly normal behavior for a man who not only wrote, directed, and produced his own play but had the temerity to attend the opening.

After the performance it is considered in perfectly good taste for strangers to walk into a dressing room, embrace an undressed performer, and shout, "Darling! You were wonderful!" Timid women in the environs of their own home act like Jezebels when visiting backstage, thinking it not at all unusual to hand a pair of pants to an unknown nude actor. Hard-headed

businessmen, tyrannical executives, professional cynics, and their dour escorts become sweet-smelling, laughing, lovable personalities as they fawn over the actors backstage, gushing, "Marvelous!" and "Too wonderful!" No one means anything he says; everybody knows it, and no one would want it any different. Honest appraisals should be saved for some other time. Now is the time, before the notices are printed, to revel in sweet success. Simulated but none the less real tears and laughter are called for on these occasions. This is not the time or place to pay casually a polite visit. Enthusiasm which constrains itself to a confining "I enjoyed it," or a ponderous "Interesting," or a quibbling "Not bad" will immediately stamp you as a yokel.

With the lowering of the final curtain, blotting out the reflected light from the stage, your fate has been sealed. Similar to a camera, your exposed negative is now in the developing process. The captured image is irretrievable; the audience has indelibly recorded the facts and the morning's press will print the results.

Do not be alarmed by the mad rush for exit doors as the curtain descends. These rushees are mostly drama critics who have, in most cases, but one hour between curtain and publication to write their reviews. Others rushing for the doors are doing so in the fond hope of being mistaken for drama critics rushing to their offices to write their reviews. The overwhelming majority and relatively saner members of the audience will remain to applaud, whistle, bang their empty candy boxes, and, with rolled-up programs serving as improvised megaphones, scream "Bravo! Bravo!" while the greenhorns yell "Author! Author!" until the house lights go up and silence them.

Alone at last you will find it impossible to remember who it was that first encouraged you with, "Say, you know, that would make a great play."

DRAWINGS

THE FOLLOWING section is a portfolio of theatre drawings selected at random—not the publishing house squired by Bennett Cerf, but the random which comes from playfully selecting a few drawings out of a pile of a couple of thousand.

Across the past thirty years, with monotonous regularity, my drawings have appeared in the drama sections of the New York *Times,* the *Herald Tribune,* the Brooklyn *Eagle,* and the old *World.* These thousands of drawings, scattered in living rooms, museums, and men's rooms across the country, had first to be located. Had I known, back in 1920, that one day there would be concerted pressure from my family and friends to publish a book in order to pay a few bills, I, of course, would have meticulously filed each original drawing under the day, month, and year of its inception. But, alas, such was not the case. The truth is that I have distributed my drawings around as promiscuously as Dr. Wharton signs, and to retrieve them for the purpose of not publishing them in this book is one of those social coups which has distinguished me in the past as the type of man not to marry. (Especially to those whose prompt response to my request has been rewarded by getting their pictures back with the frames busted.)

The second phase of correlating the assembled drawings was to eliminate those whose subject matter was unimportant or where the graphic design was of dubious quality. This weeding-out process took many weeks, leaving me exhausted, and with the same couple of thousand drawings.

In desperation I chose only Pulitzer Prize plays, Critics' Circle Award winners, Burns Mantle's yearly choice of the ten best, George Jean Nathan's pick of the crop, Brooks Atkinson's favorite plays, and Richard Watts's favorite ingénues. Digging further into the files, I exhumed drawings of many shows which drew rave notices from Benchley, Woollcott, Hammond, Anderson, and Wilella Waldorf. The drawings were beginning to pile up again: Louis Kronenberger, Gil Gabriel, Wolcott Gibbs, Eric Bentley, Rosamond Gilder. . . . More authorities: Robert Garland, Walter Winchell, John Mason Brown. . . . This can't go on. . . . Joseph Wood Krutch, Stark Young, John Gassner. . . . It's endless. . . . John Beauford, Lewis Nicols,

Louis Funke, Arthur Pollock, Kelcey Allen, Ward Morehouse, Richard Lockridge, Bob Coleman, Otis Guernsey, Claudia Cassidy. . . . Help! . . . Ashton Stevens, Elliot Norton, William F. McDermott, John Rosenfield, Sensenderfer, Linton Martin, Donald Kirkley, Mark Baron, Lawrence Perry, Hal Eaton, Rowland Field, Jack Gaver, Kappe Phelan, Richard Coe, Russell McLaughlin . . . Elinor Hughes, Robert Pollak, Richard Hobart, Harold V. Cohen, Douglas Watt, Robert Sylvester, George Freedley, Joseph Shipley, Whitney Bolton, William Hawkins, John Chapman, "Hobe" Morrison, Arthur "Bron"son. . . . It's madness—stark, raving madness. . . . I could feel myself wondering about me. . . . My wife and child seemed far away, yet near enough to be mortal enemies.

I sobbed aloud like a rejected architect. . . . I heard a voice, clear and unmistakable. It said, "Why don't you straighten yourself out? What are you, a drama critic? Forget about the shows. Who cares whether they won prizes or not? Stick to personalities! That's your field—people! Every dope knows a star when he sees one; all you've got to do is pick out the drawings of big-name stars and you've got a best-selling mug-book on your hands." I looked up from my bed of Bristol boards to discover my four-and-a-half-year-old daughter standing in the studio. Had she been telling me these seemingly obvious truths, or had my muse goosed the inner man into sanity? At any rate, I embraced my daughter and, kissing her on all four cheeks, I started with renewed, unbounded energy to make a new selection.

Let's see. . . . There's Miller and Lyles in *Rang Tang,* at the Royale; Sacha Guitry in a repertory season; Albert Carroll burlesquing Ethel Barrymore in *The Grand Street Follies;* Marie Cahill in *Merry-Go-Round;* Ed Wynn in *Manhattan Mary;* Blanche Yurka in *The Squall;* Francine Larrimore in *Chicago;* Aline MacMahon in *Maya.* . . . Why, this is a cinch. I could kick myself for not thinking of this before. . . . Joe Cook in *Rain or Shine;* Zelma O'Neal in *Good News;* Lionel Atwill in *The King Can Do No Wrong;* Pert Kelton in *The Five O'Clock Girl* . . . and to think I owe all this to my lovable, intelligent, beautiful daughter. . . . Frank Craven in *The Nineteenth Hole;* Basil Sydney and Mary Ellis in a modern-dress version of *The Taming of the Shrew;* Will Mahoney in *Take the Air;* Sir Guy Standing in *Diversion;* Guy Robertson in *Lovely Lady;* Berton Churchill in *Revelry;* Harry Lauder in a four-week farewell appearance at the Knickerbocker; Billy B. Van in *Sunny Days;* Billie Yarbo in *Keep Shufflin';* Alison Skipworth in *Say When;* Bill Robinson in *Blackbirds;* Charles King in *Present Arms;* Florence Reed in *The Shanghai Gesture;* Basil Rathbone in *The Command to Love.* . . .

The drawings are beginning to pile up again. . . . Holbrook Blinn in *The Play's the Thing;* Jane Cowl in *The Road to Rome.* . . . Where did I go wrong? . . . Effie Shannon in *Her Unborn Child.* . . . If I ever get my hands on that repulsive child of mine . . . Gus Shy in . . .

When I came to, clutching a handful of beard, the unmistakable voice seemed to say, "Now, wait a minute, Hirschfeld. Relax! All these drawings are only from one year—1927. At the rate you're piling them up you'll be way over the thousand mark before you reach 1940. Take it easy. Go away for a while. Simmer down!" I looked up, expecting once again to confront my daughter, but this time there was no one there. So that's it, eh? Talking to myself. Well, it won't be long now before they back up the wagon and haul me out of here in a suit buttoned down the back. . . . I fought back the impulse to run home to Mom. My thoughts strayed to happier, more carefree days . . . Bali, Siam, St. Louis . . . when suddenly I was held firmly in a grip of euphoria. The crudely lettered words ZAM! BANG! POWIE! were erased and replaced with a badly drawn electric bulb in the balloon of my thoughts. The caption under the bulb read, "Why not confine *your* selection to the *outstanding* theatre *personality* of *each* year?" Seemed reasonable: thirty years, thirty drawings. . . . Simple, direct, easily comprehended; no monkey business. . . . I once again started to compile the list.

Let's see, we'll start with, say, 1935 . . . there's Helen Hayes, the Lunts; 1936, Katharine Cornell, the Lunts; 1937, Helen Hayes, Katharine Cornell; 1939, the Lunts, Helen Hayes; 1940 . . .

The following section is a portfolio of drawings selected at random.

The following caption appeared in the New York Times:

> *Here are a group of people who are connected with the playing of* The Admiral Had a Wife, *which opens on Wednesday. Reading in the usual order, they are E. J. Ballantine, Richard Hale, Alfred Drake, Martha Hodge, Uta Hagen, and Peter Goo Chong. The comedy will arrive at the Playhouse.*

The Times *was wrong. This play never opened at the Playhouse or anywhere else because the Japanese corroborated the playwright's thesis, of decadence and corruption in the administration of Pearl Harbor, by blowing up the harbor on the day this drawing was published, December 7, 1941.*

Victor Jory, Dame May Whitty, and Eva Le Gallienne in Therese.
Biltmore Theatre, October 9, 1945.

Freddie Trenkler in the 1944 Ice Show at the Center Theatre—Hats Off to Ice *(a title borrowed, I presume, from the editorial pages of the late lamented P.M., whose editors daily congratulated each other in a polite column titled "Hats Off").*

Balcony upper left—a madman sprays the audience with popcorn while another holds a pair of rabbits aloft and screams "Harvey!" A wailing midget disguised as an infant dangles from an upper box. Members of the audience are persuaded by the chorus girls to dance in the aisles with their pants rolled up. Frank Libuse, uninhibited entertainer, may be seen sitting on my shoulder as I laboriously try to record

the proceedings. A zany pit orchestra equipped with insulated fright wigs are beaten over the head by the conductor, who wields a baseball bat for a baton. On stage, Olsen and Johnson, the originators of Hellzapoppin, *shoot off revolvers and toss real eggs at the audience while a living statue of the "Thinker" sits immobile, silently contemplating these insane goings on at the Winter Garden, September 22, 1938.*

Ethel Waters and Josh White in the all-Negro show Blue Holiday. *Belasco Theatre, May 18, 1945.*

Dolly Haas in Lute Song. Plymouth Theatre, June 18, 1946.

Gene Sheldon, Lou Holtz, Paul Draper, Hazel Scott, and Willie Howard in Priorities of 1942.

Helen Hayes and daughter Mary toured the summer theatre circuit in Alice-Sit-by-the-Fire, opening in the Bucks County Playhouse, July 29, 1946.

Martita Hunt and Estelle Winwood, two extravagantly sane women,
in The Madwoman of Chaillot, *December 27, 1948.*

Mothers on Broadway, 1949. L to R: Viola Keats, Anne of the Thousand Days; *Dorothy Stickney,* Life with Mother; *Mildred Dunnock,* Death of a Salesman; *Adrianne Allen,* Edward My Son; *and Phyllis Povah,* Light Up the Sky.

A *schoolgirl, a party girl, society's pet,* and a femme fatale *engaged in espionage for a foreign power are portrayed by Beatrice Lillie in* Set to Music. *Broadhurst Theatre, November 18, 1938.*

Michael Redgrave and Flora Robson—Macbeth and his Lady—are
counseled by the Three Voices—Robinson Stone, Martin Balsam,
and Harry Hess—in Macbeth. After an out-of-town tryout in To-
ronto, Canada, it opened in New York at the National Theatre,
March 31, 1948.

Godfrey Tearle and Katharine Cornell in Anthony and Cleopatra.
Martin Beck Theatre, November 26, 1947.

Ed Wynn in a 1940 revue at the Broadhurst Theatre, Boys and Girls Together.

Mae West bares her ankle in Diamond Lil, *February 5, 1949.*

Sophie Tucker—"the last of the red-hot mamas"—in Leave It to Me.
Imperial Theatre, September 12, 1939. Further theatrical history
was made this year by two unrelated incidents: Garbo laughed and
the Federal Theatre died.

Alfred Lunt and Lynn Fontanne in The Taming of the Shrew, *Guild Theatre, September 30, 1935.*

Ethel Merman as Annie Oakley in Annie Get Your Gun, *Imperial
Theatre, May 16, 1946.*

Jean Arthur, in the title role of Peter Pan, takes to the air escaping the clichés of the sinister Captain Hook, portrayed by Boris Karloff, April 24, 1950.

Dolly Haas, Lillian Gish, and John Gielgud in Crime and Punishment, *December 22, 1947.*

Fred Allen, the only writer in the world who has written more than he can lift.

Sara Allgood, Barry Fitzgerald, and Arthur Shields in Juno and the
Paycock. National Theatre, January 16, 1940.

119

Frank Fay in Harvey *(Pulitzer Prize Play);* Laurette Taylor *in* The
Glass Menagerie *(Critics' Circle Award Winner);* Judy Holliday *in*
Kiss Them for Me *and* Frederick O'Neal *in* Anna Lucasta *(Best
Supporting Roles of Season, 1944-1945).*

José Ferrer in The Silver Whistle, *November, 1948.*

By placing your hand over the right profile you will expose the face of Jimmy Savo; blotting out the profile of Savo you will reveal the likeness of Teddy Hart. This department of utter confusion reflects graphically their mistaken identity roles as the Dremio Twins in The Boys From Syracuse. Alvin Theatre, December 12, 1938.

George Gershwin's Porgy and Bess, *revived at the Majestic Theatre,
January 21, 1942.*

Two G.B.S. plays running concurrently on Broadway were the occasion for this incongruous mingling of the characters from both shows—The Devil's Disciple, January 25, 1950, and Caesar and Cleopatra, December 21, 1949—in an imagined Shavian cocktail party. Reading in the usual order, they are Bertha Belmore (Ftatateeta), Victor Jory (Anthony

Anderson), Lilli Palmer (Cleopatra), John Buckmaster (Apollodorus),
Maurice Evans (Dick Dudgeon), Bernard Shaw (Himself), Nicholas Joy
(Pothinus), Arthur Treacher (Britannus), Ivan Simpson (Theodotus),
Marsha Hunt (Judith Anderson), Cedric Hardwicke (Caesar), Ralph
Forbes (Rufio), and Dennis King (General Burgoyne).

126

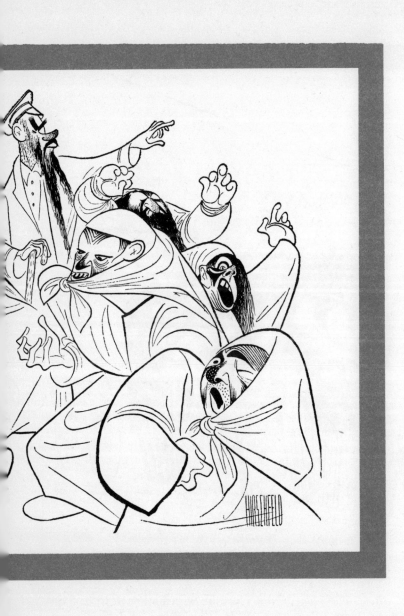

The "dance of the beggars" in The Dybbuk, *which the Habima Players brought from Israel to the Broadway Theatre for a limited engagement. Hanna Rovina is the actress in the center, May 22, 1948.*

Some of those who played Father in Life with Father. *L to R: Stanley Ridges, Harry Bannister, A. H. Van Buren, Edwin Cooper, Percy Waram, Howard Lindsay, and Louis Calhern. Empire Theatre, 1939-1948.*

Percy Waram and Leo G. Carroll in The Late George Apley, *November 23, 1944.*

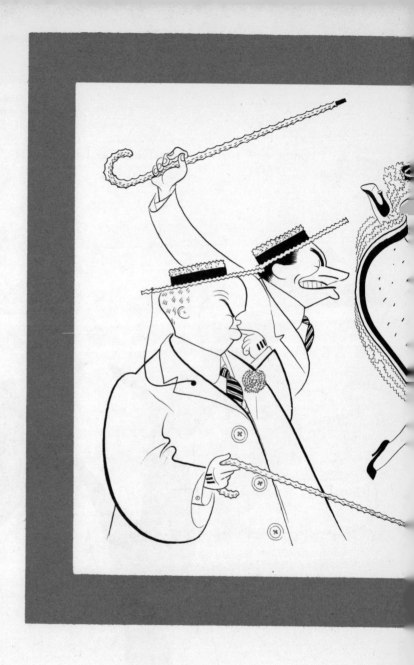

Another attempt to bring back vaudeville in 1942 came and went under the legend Keep 'Em Laughing, *with Victor Moore, William Gaxton, the Hartmans, Hildegarde, and Jack Cole.*

Orson Welles as Brutus in a modern-dress version of Julius Caesar.
The Mercury Theatre, November 6, 1937.

June Havoc in the title role of Sadie Thompson, *a musical based on* Rain, *presented November 16, 1944, at the Alvin Theatre.*

133

Henry Hull, one of the many Jeeter Lesters in the highly successful
Tobacco Road. *This play ran so long that they eventually grew
their own turnips on the stage of the Forty-eighth Street Theatre,
1933-1941.*

Jimmy Durante carries on a heated discussion with himself in the musical Red, Hot and Blue. *The Winter Garden, March 18, 1937.*

Leo Carroll, Faith Brook, Tom Helmore, Frieda Inescort, Patricia Kirkland, Walter Hudd, Nigel Stock, and Ralph Forbes in You Never Can Tell. *Martin Beck Theatre, March 16, 1948.*

The Critics' Circle meet at the Hotel Algonquin to choose the Best Play of 1941. L to R: Rosamund Gilder (Theatre Arts), *Joseph Wood Krutch* (Nation), *Richard Watts* (New York Herald Tribune), *John Mason Brown* (Post), *Walter Winchell* (Daily Mirror), *George Jean Nathan* (American Mercury), *Sidney Whipple* (New York World-Telegram), *Brooks Atkinson* (New York Times), *Arthur Pol-*

lock (Brooklyn Eagle), *Grenville Vernon* (Commonweal), *Stark Young* (New Republic), *Wolcott Gibbs* (New Yorker), *Burns Mantle* (Daily News), *Richard Lockridge* (Sun), *Louis Kronenberger* (P.M.), *Kelcey Allen* (Women's Wear Daily), *Oliver Claxton* (Cue), *John Anderson* (New York Journal-American), *John Gassner* (Direction).

One Touch of Venus *opened October 7, 1943, at the Imperial Theatre with Sono Osata, Mary Martin, Teddy Hart (down there at the bottom), Kenny Baker, John Boles, and Paula Laurence.*

ABOUT THE AUTHOR

Far be it from us to suggest that Al Hirschfeld's wit is razor sharp because he wrote and illustrated Show Business Is No Business *sitting in a barber chair, but the fact remains that Mr. Hirschfeld's favorite work spot is the kind of seat usually found in what were once called tonsorial parlors. This one is in his large studio atop the house he lives in with his wife, actress Dolly Haas, and small daughter. In it he has turned out thousands of drawings well known to readers of* The New York Times, Holiday, Vanity Fair, Redbook, Collier's, Seventeen, Theatre Arts, Life, *and many other magazines, as well as to visitors to a number of this country's art museums.*

Al Hirschfeld was born in St. Louis, Missouri, moved to New York at an early age and has, since then, spent considerable time in world-wide travel. His companion on his last trip around the world in 1947 was S. J. Perelman; their misadventures are immortalized in Westward, Ha! *In New York, Mr. Hirschfeld's special beat, since 1922, has been the area around Shubert Alley.*